WINTER IN MOSCOW

by
MALCOLM
MUGGERIDGE

WILLIAM B. EERDMANS PUBLISHING COMPANY
GRAND RAPIDS, MICHIGAN

Copyright © 1934, 1987 by Thomas Malcolm Muggeridge

First published 1934 by Eyre and Spottiswoode, London, and Little Brown, Boston. This edition published 1987 by Wm. B. Eerdmans Publishing Co.
255 Jefferson Ave. SE, Grand Rapids, MI 49503.

All rights reserved
Printed in the United States of America

Library of Congress Cataloging-in-Publication Data

Muggeridge, Malcolm, 1903-
   Winter in Moscow.

    1. Soviet Union — History — Revolution, 1917-1921 — Fiction. I. Title.
PR6025.U5W5   1987   823'.912   87-9170

ISBN 0-8028-2063-X

CONTENTS

	INTRODUCTION	vii
	PREFACE	7
I.	REVOLUTIONARIES	17
II.	PROLETARIAN MYSTICISM	53
III.	HEAVY INDUSTRY	89
IV.	ASH-BLOND INCORRUPTIBLE	125
V.	COLOUR STUFF	159
VI.	DIPLOMATIC INCIDENT	185
VII.	WHO WHOM?	207

INTRODUCTION

MICHAEL D. AESCHLIMAN

FIRST published in 1934, Malcolm Muggeridge's novel *Winter in Moscow* is based on his experiences as a correspondent for the *Manchester Guardian* in Russia in 1932 and 1933. A. J. P. Taylor, one of the finest English historians of our time, wrote in 1965 that this novel was "probably the best book ever written on Soviet Russia."[1] In the light of the appearance of Aleksandr Solzhenitsyn's *Gulag Archipelago* in the 1970s, and of other dissident, underground Russian classics such as Andrei Sinyavsky's *A Voice from the Chorus* and Nadezhda Mandelstam's *Hope against Hope* and *Hope Abandoned*, this verdict surely needs revision, as Muggeridge would be the first to admit. In fact he hoped for and predicted the emergence of this great Russian literature of political and spiritual protest and moral documentation, writing in *Time and Tide* in 1937: "Perhaps a new literature will come to pass in Russia.... If so, it will be a literature of revolt and so anathema to the Soviet Establishment. Perhaps it is being scribbled even now in concentration camps and other dark corridors."[2] Over forty years later, speaking in London to help promote a film on the life and writing of Solzhenitsyn, who by this time had established with undeniable documentation, scope, and literary power the horrifying history and facts of Soviet tyranny to which Muggeridge had steadily tried to draw attention in the intervening years, Muggeridge said that in our "murky time, Solzhenitsyn represents everything that is noble and wonderful in human life and in the human mind. . . . He is a very great man."[3]

But Taylor's generous estimate of *Winter in Moscow*, which elsewhere he calls a "masterpiece,"[4] needs revision and explanation rather than abandonment, for reasons at once literary and historical. Like this great writing of Solzhenitsyn, Sinyavsky, and Mandelstam, *Winter in Moscow* is both imaginative and documentary, and it imaginatively documents realities with which the "progressive" Western intelligentsia is still terribly uneasy. The belief in an inevitable, collective human progress grew to dominate "enlightened" Western opinion more and more steadily from the time of Bacon in the seventeenth century, through the propagandistic and revolutionary writing of the French *philosophes* and their Jacobin and socialist successors in the eighteenth and early nineteenth centuries until, by the mid-nineteenth century, as Hannah Arendt has written, it "became an almost universally accepted dogma."[5] "Glory to Man in the highest!" wrote the poet A. C. Swinburne (1837-1909), expressing the characteristic optimism and the utopian expectations of his era, which the title of one of his collections, *Songs before Sunrise*, conveniently illustrates.

The massive carnage of the First World War was a terrible blow to these expectations of progressive "sunrise," especially in their liberal, gradualist, painless version, and the onset of the Great Depression from 1929 was still more damaging. But both events had the effect for the secularized intelligentsia of making more credible the Marxist, catastrophist version of progress. That version also promised an ultimate earthly utopia, but insisted that it could not be achieved painlessly, insisted that things would have to get worse before getting better, that war and revolution of indeterminate duration and destructiveness would necessarily intervene, that an omelette could not be made without breaking eggs, to use one of the favored analogies.

In what seemed to many the final, mortal crisis of an obviously corrupt and declining world of Western industrial capitalism, the appeal and credibility of Marxism, its Word apparently now made flesh by the Russian Revolution in its Bolshevik regime, grew enormously, especially after 1929, and especially because the Marxist regime promoted itself with the mystique of the great God-word that had powered the idea of collective progress from its very beginnings: science. Marxism claimed to be a "science," Marx priding himself on having discovered the scientific "laws of history" in the same way that he believed Darwin had discovered the laws of "natural selection" and biology.[6] Both theories are grossly reductive and mechanistic, but were and are easily popularized by the "terrible simplifiers" of the modern era.[7] Thus while the liberal hope of painless progress, steady and sure, had been rendered incredible by the catastrophic events of 1914 to 1930, the promoters of Marxist Russian "scientific socialism" grew enormously in credibility. The English Labour politician and later cabinet minister, John Strachey (1901-1963), for example, typically wrote in 1936 that the Communist Party was "the only body of persons who possess a knowledge of the science of social change";[8] this at the time when the great show trials and the murderous purges were taking place in the "workers' paradise."

In one of the Moscow diaries (6 January 1933) on which *Winter in Moscow* was to be based, Muggeridge, who had himself read natural sciences at Cambridge as an undergraduate, already acidulously noted one of the chief flaws in such thinking: "People who go all out for the scientific outlook end by producing the greatest of all absurdities — mysticized science; the worship of something idiotic like the Five Year Plan."[9] The critique of the deterministic mystique of an omnicompetent science had been a chief feature of much of the great literature of the nineteenth century, as in Dostoyevsky, to whose lonely and untended grave Muggeridge was to pay a visit on his way out of Russia: "pseudo-science", Dostoyevsky wrote, is a "terrible scourge of mankind, a scourge worse than plague, famine, and war. . . . Half-knowledge is a tyrant without precedent."[10] As the grisly effects of the Five Year Plans, despite all their falsified statistics, were to show, Dostoyevsky was right. "A percentage!" he wrote elsewhere, "What fine words they use, to be sure! So soothing. Scientific. All you have to do is to say 'percentage' and all your worries are over."[11] Grossly inflated and faked statistics, unavailable to confirmation by independent scrutiny, were to have an enormous propagandistic effect. As Freda Utley, having lived in the early 1930s in Russia, was to write: "Communists and fellow-travellers, many of whom had never seen the inside of a factory or power station, journalists and authors, . . . 'intellectuals' of all kinds, came on conducted tours of the Soviet Union and worshipped before the shrine of the machine."[12] This gross credulity of the intellectuals astounded Muggeridge, and he was never to forget it.

The criticism of this credulity and of the illusions of "mysticized science" were to become themes of Muggeridge's polemical and satirical writing for the rest of his life, steadily asserted, meditated, and applied, in season and out, for over fifty years. Like Disraeli in the century before, he knew early on that "the fallacy of the great utilitarian scheme consists in confounding wisdom with knowledge,"[13] and that as hard to get as wisdom was, science was not and never could be the chief means whereby it could be gotten. Though Aldous Huxley and C. S. Lewis were to make the same point with great eloquence and rational power, their voices and Muggeridge's were to be minority ones, for to abandon faith in the omnicompetence of science seemed to many like abandoning faith in the meaningfulness of the human enterprise, in the progressive future itself.

And this faith in the secular utopia of the future, being brought about by "scientific socialism" and applied science (endlessly propagated in Russia in mind-numbing propagandistic slogans such as "socialism + electrification = communism"), had all the propagandistic advantages available to those who make of science a religion. Speaking of Soviet Russia, the influential American publicist Lincoln Steffens (1866-1936) said, "I have seen the future, and it works"; but William C. Bullitt, the American diplomat with whom Steffens traveled to Russia in 1919, later asserted that Steffens "was rehearsing this formula long before seeing Lenin's Russia."[14] Steffens continued to reiterate it after returning, and it became a famous promotional adage. For many Western intellectuals, in fact, this sentiment became a creed, not to be deserted or even amended in light of even the messiest and most obvious contradictions of it by empirical evidence, by the actual facts of history. Utopia was expected and longed for, utopia was promised, utopia was believed to be an inevitable and rapid, if occasionally clumsy, process of formation.

From 1930 to 1932, Muggeridge lived and worked in Manchester. The son of a moderate Socialist member of

Parliament, related by marriage to the Fabian Webbs, and himself a brilliant young left-wing journalist in Lancashire, the depressed heartland of British industry, he was in a prime position and frame of mind to entertain, understand, and sympathize with the Marxist view that was taking so much of the intellectual world by storm. Although not yet thirty years old, Muggeridge had already spent periods living and working in both India and Egypt, where he hated the snobbish, self-interested, and moribund remnants of imperialism and sympathized with the radical and national aspirations of the colonial peoples. Back in England as a journalist and editorialist on the famous liberal *Manchester Guardian* he saw, or seemed to see, close up in Lancashire the collapse and death-throes of that capitalist industrial order that Britian had pioneered and that had taken her to world economic preeminence over the previous century and a half. The Marxist analysis of the crisis of capitalism could not fail to be impressive.

But in addition to the indubitable analytical and diagnostic powers of Marxism, their apparent accuracy to the depressed and declining state of Britain and the West generally, and the utopian promise they held out in the indeterminate but inevitable future, Muggeridge noted early on — with more ambivalence, like his American contemporary Reinhold Niebuhr — a ruthlessly realistic assessment in Marxism of power relations, an assessment that seemed superior to liberal moralism at least in its accuracy and honesty. But it was on this issue of power, along with his disbelief in the "mysticized scientism" aspect of Marxism, that a strong antipathy was at work in the young Muggeridge's developing moral sensibility. He knew that "Who whom?" was Lenin's great question: "At bottom, the question of control,"

Lenin wrote, "is really the question: Who is it that exercises control? . . . What class controls and what class is controlled?" But in Muggeridge's fidelity to the lived and observed experience of his own stay in Russia, he came to see something quite unexpectedly, monstrously different from the Marxist vision of the control of class over class. He came to see that the Nietzschean "will to power" of a fanatical, amoral intellectual sect, the Bolsheviks, was really at work, far more ruthlessly and exploitively than the hypocritical, fitful, unorganized social Darwinistic scramble of Bounderbys and Babbitts in the ramshackle capitalist democracies. The Bolsheviks had established not a "Dictatorship of the Proletariat," but a dictatorship *over* the proletariat, and over everyone else too; and first Lenin, then Stalin, established a dictatorship over the Bolsheviks themselves. In later years Muggeridge would never tire of adducing and praising Blake's lines on the course of the French Revolution. Blake, he wrote, "saw that Caesar's poisoned crown would just adorn another brow":[15]

> The hand of vengeance found the Bed
> To which the Purple Tyrant fled;
> The iron hand crushed the Tyrant's head
> And became a tyrant in his stead.

But Muggeridge learned to make this distinction, which Heller and Nekrich have recently noted: "A comparison of the numbers of victims in . . . 200 years of tsarist rule and a few years of Stalinist collectivization shows the difference between autocracy and totalitarianism, between an unhurried historical existence and an insane rush towards 'progress'."[16]

Already when he was in Moscow, Muggeridge was

meditating, trying to think through the paternity, the provenance, of this modern horror, which could throw up as its leader a technologically proficient murderer and sadist such as Stalin, a scientific-socialist Genghis Khan. Marx, A. J. P. Taylor was later to write, "was a rationalist, believing in Progress and anxious to discover its laws," whereas "Lenin belonged to the age of collective man and of the struggle for power. . . . He wanted to know how to get to the right end of a gun and stay there."[17] With his already profound sensitivity to political and ethical realities, Muggeridge saw this in Russia early and accurately. Reviewing his *Diaries* many years later, Taylor wrote that Muggeridge "was disillusioned overnight and has retained . . . one fixed principle: a hatred of power-worshippers, particularly of the Communist variety."[18] Already on 15 January 1933 Muggeridge confided to his diary in Moscow: "If I had ever had any doubts about the existence of evil, this place would have convinced me!"[19] And in the first volume of what undeniably *is* his masterpiece, and one of the great works of literature published in our language during the last half century, Muggeridge's autobiographical *Chronicles of Wasted Time*, he reports a remark that one of the Communist censors with whom he had constantly clashed in Moscow made to him not long before he left Russia. The censor "had, he said, formed the impression that when I first came to the USSR . . . I believed in nothing, whereas I went away believing in something."[20]

That "something" was the reality of evil, and the willing collaboration with it by legions of adulatory liberal and socialist intellectuals was something that would never cease to astonish and appall him, and would never cease to inspire his pen to some of the sharpest, most powerful moral satire ever written in our language. The satire on "learned foolishness" has a long history in Western literature, from St. Paul's comment on the feckless neophilia of the Athenian intellectuals in Acts 17, through Cicero's "I missed my end, and lost my way,/ By crackbrain'd wisdom led astray," to Swift's mockery of scientific and utopian intellectuals in *Gulliver's Travels*. But the ferocious, caustic Juvenalian satire on the "treason of the intellectuals" in our own era, on their widespread and willing collaboration with and worship of varieties of tyranny, especially Communist, is one of the chief, enduringly valid, antiseptic features of Muggeridge's writing, and it begins in *Winter in Moscow*.

The literature on this intellectual folly and treason is by now very large and some of it is of very high quality — one thinks of Solzhenitsyn, of David Caute's *The Fellow Travellers*, judiciously subtitled "A Postscript to the Enlightenment," of Andrew Boyle's book on the Cambridge spies, of much of George Orwell's writing, and, in a more general mode, of the magnificent recent *Utopia in Power: The History of the Soviet Union from 1917 to the Present* (1982) by the emigré Russian historians Mikhail Heller and Aleksandr Nekrich. Aldous Huxley and George Orwell, partly inspired by the Russian Zamyatin's novel *We*, took the satire on scientistic utopias and power-worshipping intellectuals to great heights.

Muggeridge pioneered this literature, though profound individual insights into the new era of collective, "scientific" tyranny had been made by Russian writers such as Ivan Bunin and Zamyatin, insights such as Zamyatin's 1920 assertion that "we have lived through the epoch of suppression of the masses," but now "we are living in an epoch of suppression of the individual in the name of the masses."[21] What Muggeridge saw in Russia was the suppression of both masses (dictatorship *over* the proletariat, "dekulakization") *and* individuals ("liquidation of bourgeois elements," "class enemies"), a process that was to be repeated in Nazi Germany and in all the Communist offspring—China, Vietnam, Cambodia, Cuba, and Nicaragua—and that was to be aided, abetted, and praised by "progressive" "political pilgrims" again and again.

The idolization of Stalin by Western intellectuals had already begun by the time Muggeridge reached Russia in 1932, as it would later occur with Mao Tse-Tung, Ho Chi Minh, and Fidel Castro—not to speak of the adulation by right-wing power-worshipping intellectuals of Mussolini and Hitler. But "the judgments on Stalin, if collected," the great historian of Soviet Russia Leonard Schapiro has recently written, "would present such a catalogue of the folly of intellectuals as ought to prevent those of us who claim to belong to this category from ever raising our voices again."[22] Bernard Shaw, the Webbs, H. G. Wells, André Gide, Henri Barbusse—the list is long and distinguished, and Muggeridge would never forget this "trahison des clercs" and would try to publicize it throughout his life as an object lesson.

"Disillusionment with Communism, dismay at the methods of the Soviet Union, are nowadays such familiar themes," Anthony Powell wrote in his 1980 memoir *Faces in My Time*,

> that the force of Muggeridge's virtually one-man onslaught in the 1930s is hard to grasp for those who did not experience those years. The Muggeridge impact, for its cogency to be appreciated, must be understood in relation to the intellectual atmosphere of the period.

This atmosphere was one in which "many people were apt to think of what was happening in Russia as no worse than a few rich people being relieved of their surplus cash," Powell continued,

> a proceeding of which some approved, some disapproved. True, there were awkward stories about executions, torture, forced labour, government-engineered famine, but the analogy of omelettes and eggs would often be invoked by those who approved; while those who disapproved were suspected of doing so for the wrong reasons, that is to say, desire to keep their own money.[23]

A crucial fact about Muggeridge's status, background, and attitudes, which was to have large consequence throughout his career, is here relevant: he was not mainly or merely self-interested, as so many of the conservative critics of Communism clearly were, with their privileged economic and social status obviously menaced. Long before our time Kant had formulated the immemorially old point that the "radical evil" that must be avoided by self-conscious rational and moral beings is the use of the language of ethics as a screen for self-interest or self-love, and too much bourgeois moralism has always been vulnerable to this charge, a charge that Christianity has made intermittently against the rich, powerful, and proud down through the ages and that Marxism has effectively and often accurately made ever since its origin. It has also taken the form of satire on bourgeois self-interest, especially in French literature and art: "You were hungry, but that's no excuse," says the complacently fat bourgeois magistrate to the obviously starving thief brought in manacles before him in one of Daumier's great caricatures; "I too get hungry every day, but I don't go stealing."[24] Anatole France talked about the "majestic egalitarianism of the law, which forbids rich and poor alike to sleep under bridges, to beg in the streets, and to steal bread," and he defined justice as "the means by which established injustices are sanctioned."[25] But long before this, in *King Lear*, Shakespeare knew that if you "plate sin with gold . . . the lance of justice hurtless breaks." With the depth and accuracy of this critique Muggeridge was familiar, and he also knew, and would know again, what it was to be poor. He was neither born nor bred in the camp of the wealthy and glamorous and never had much admiration for their values or aspiration for their style of life. Thus his exposé of the "workers' paradise lost" could not easily be dismissed as bourgeois self-interest. Like Reinhold Niebuhr and T. S. Eliot, he saw these things disinterestedly, in the light of elementary justice and truth, and he wrote about them with a moral sensitivity and eloquence both deep and sure.

Favored relation of the Fabian Webbs, son of a Socialist MP, writer for a prominent liberal journal, Muggeridge had had a sympathetic grasp of Marxism and had gone to Russia in 1932 favorably — though not uncritically — disposed to its institutionalization. What he saw there immediately appalled him by its fraudulence, hypocrisy, tyranny, and ferocity. The censorship horrified him and filled him with bitter irony toward the happy collaboration with it by so many Western journalists. The most notable among them was the *New York Times's* Walter Duranty (satirized in *Winter in Moscow* as Jefferson), who won a Pulitzer Prize in 1932 for deceitfully propagandistic dispatches from Russia that routinely denied or minimized horrors he knew to have taken place. Muggeridge was later to write that Duranty was "the greatest liar of any journalist I have met in fifty years of journalism."[26] Yet Duranty and the British Communist Claud Cockburn helped to shape Franklin Roosevelt's impression of Soviet Russia as "progressive." He recognized the Soviet Union diplomatically and sent "the corrupt and gullible Joseph Davies" as ambassador to Moscow in 1936 "with instructions to win Stalin's friendship at all costs."[27] Robert Conquest writes:

> At a banquet at the Waldorf Astoria to celebrate the recognition of the USSR by the United States, a list of names was read, each politely applauded by the guests until Walter Duranty's was reached; then, Alexander Woollcott wrote in the *New Yorker*, "the one really prolonged pandemonium was evoked.... Indeed, one got the impression that America, in a spasm of discernment, was recognizing both Russia and Walter Duranty." Well, a spasm anyway.[28]

What Duranty and innumerable other journalists and "political pilgrims" lied about was not only the commonplace censorship and tyranny of life in Moscow, not only the clearly apparent secrecy, brutality, and deceitfulness of the governing *apparat* headed by Stalin. More specifically, tangibly, and tragically, they lied about, by denying that it happened, one of the greatest mass crimes of human history — what is summed up in the title of Robert Conquest's definitive recent book, *Harvest of Sorrow: Soviet Collectivization and the Terror-Famine*. The forced collectivization of Russian agriculture in the Ukraine and adjacent areas, initiated by Stalin as part of the first "Five Year Plan"—from which Russian agriculture has never recovered—is described by Heller and Nekrich, in appropriately anticipatory language, as the "first socialist genocide": "The genocide against the peasants in the Soviet Union was unique not only for its monstrous scale; it was directed against an indigenous population by a government of the same nationality, and in time of peace."[29] Robert Conquest quotes Khrushchev, one of the chief henchmen, as saying that "people were dying in enormous numbers."[30] Heller and Nekrich note that in the attempt at "dekulakization" (that is, the elimination or exile of industrious peasants) and forced collectivization "regular units of the Red Army, backed by air power, were thrown against the peasantry." One of those who directed the suppression of the peasants "reported to a meeting of the Politburo that the rivers of the Northern Caucasus were carrying thousands of corpses to the sea."[31] Conquest estimates that in the period 1930 to 1937, fourteen and a half million people were thus killed or forcibly starved to death in the breadbasket of Russia by their own government. This is a figure comparable to the World Wars and greater by far than the Nazi holocaust of Jews and Poles.[32]

In what may be said to be the turning point in Muggeridge's life, he managed to elude supervision in Moscow and to travel by train throughout the Ukraine and the Northern Caucasus in early 1933. What he saw would never be forgotten and would inspire a lifetime of writing, characterized by a sustained moral urgency and seriousness unexcelled in modern English letters. By witnessing horrible, indubitable evil, the brilliant skeptic and rebel became a literary moralist, like his later friend George Orwell. "This particular famine," Muggeridge wrote, "was planned and deliberate; not due to any natural catastrophe like failure of rain, or cyclone, or flooding. An administrative famine brought about by the forced collectivization of agriculture; an assault on the countryside by party *apparatchiks* . . . supported by strong-arm squads from the military and the police."[33]

Back in Moscow, he managed to get his dispatches past the Russian censors by sending them out in the British diplomatic bag.

> As I wrote in *The Guardian*, in the course of three articles of mine that appeared on 25, 27, and 28 March 1933: "To say that there is famine in some of the most fertile parts of Russia is to say much less than the truth; there is not only famine, but a state of war, a military occupation."

He wrote of seeing "peasants with their hands tied behind them being loaded into cattle trucks at gun-point." In the final chapter of the first volume of his great autobiography ("The most compelling . . . in our century," in Prof. G. B. Tennyson's words), *The Green Stick*, Muggeridge discusses the experience of seeing all of this and of writing about it, and the results: "Reading the articles over again, they seem very inadequate in conveying the horror of it all," but as "no other foreign journalist had been into the famine areas of the USSR except under official auspices and supervision . . . my account was . . . exclusive."[34] It was also greeted in the West with widespread disbelief and accusations that he was a liar. He lost not only his post in Moscow, of course, but upon returning to London found it impossible to get journalistic employment. "Honesty is praised," Juvenal had written eighteen hundred years before, "and left to shiver."

Even *The Guardian* was clearly unhappy with his dispatches. As Max Beloff was to write in *Encounter* forty years later (May 1974), "Muggeridge was censored editorially as well as censured, and he resigned. . . . [But] on the substance of what was going on in Russia, Muggeridge was right and *The Guardian* was wrong." Back in London in 1934, Muggeridge found it impossible to get a decent job as a journalist: "My reports from Russia, and *Winter in Moscow*," he recently wrote, "had dismayed the liberal consensus, which still looked upon the Communist 'experiment' with a tolerant eye."[35] In its own way, this was another revelation.

Thus were born the vocation, the voice, the tone, and the genres that were to be characteristic of Muggeridge for more than half a century: the documentary memoir or essay or review, with strong elements of satire and philosophical and moral meditation, often by turns sermonic and comical, always characterized by the sombre sincerity of the witness who is also a wit and who, like Lear's fool, must use irony to accommodate and maintain in balance different kinds of degrees of truth, and the surfaces as well as the depths of life. He would never forget the flaccidity, the fecklessness, and the treason of the Western intelligentsia in the face of Communism; he could never forget the fate of its victims, which he had seen personally.

Some comments of Hilton Kramer in a fine essay of a decade ago on Solzhenitsyn and the other great Russian dissident writers who began to be translated in the 1970s are also true of Muggeridge, their precursor: he makes the "progressive" mind "uneasy"; he is "clearly not a liberal"; "he is not a man of the Enlightenment."

He even has the audacity to entertain doubts about *our* moral fiber. Above all, he has some harsh, categorical things to say about the Russian Revolution. He is not inclined to let us forget that it was the hero of the Revolution, Lenin, not Stalin or Hitler, who first established the most despicable political institution of modern times, the concentration camp.[36]

Above all, Muggeridge, like Solzhenitsyn, reminds his reader of the prerogative and the duty of the individual soul: to know the truth, to serve the good, however darkly visible; to try to live decently and honorably in a "murky age" rife with fraud, lies, horror, and varieties of barbarism, whether narcotic commercial nihilism or lethal communist tyranny.

Truth inwardly apprehended and expressed as art is what we have in *Winter in Moscow*, an unjustly neglected book, which A. J. P. Taylor was quite right to call a masterpiece.

NOTES

1. A. J. P. Taylor, *English History, 1914-1945* (London, 1965), quoted by Taylor in *Encounter*, April 1979, p. 94.
2. Quoted by Ian Hunter in *Malcom Muggeridge: A Life* (London, 1980), p. 90.
3. From the text of a speech, "Solzhenitsyn and the Consensus," Muggeridge delivered at the Royal Overseas League, 4 December 1980.
4. A. J. P. Taylor, review of *Like It Was: The Diaries of Malcolm Muggeridge, The Observer* (London), 29 March 1981, p. 33.
5. Hannah Arendt, *Crisis of the Republic* (New York, 1972), pp. 127-28.

6. Isaiah Berlin, *Marx* (London, 1963), p. 232.
7. For argument and documentation of this point, see Jacques Barzun, *Darwin, Marx, Wagner: Critique of a Heritage* (2nd ed., Chicago, 1958).
8. John Strachey, *The Theory and Practice of Socialism* (London, 1936), p. 237.
9. Malcolm Muggeridge, *Like It Was: A Selection from the Diaries of Malcolm Muggeridge*, ed. John Bright-Holmes (London, 1981), p. 62.
10. Fyodor Dostoyevsky, *The Possessed*, tr. A. R. MacAndrew (New York, 1962, p. 237).
11. Fyodor Dostoyevsky, *Crime and Punishment*, tr. D. Magarshack (New York, 1951), p. 69.
12. Freda Utley, *Lost Illusion* (London, 1949), p. 164.
13. Benjamin Disraeli, *Whigs and Whiggism*, quoted in John Holloway, *The Victorian Sage* (London, 1953), p. 5.
14. Quoted in Justin Kaplan, *Lincoln Steffens* (New York, 1975), chap. 13.
15. Malcolm Muggeridge, *A Third Testament* (London, 1976), p. 82.
16. Mikhail Heller and Aleksandr Nekrich, *Utopia in Power: The History of the Soviet Union from 1917 to the Present* (1982; Eng. tr. New York, 1986), p. 243.
17. A. J. P. Taylor, "Marx and Lenin," in *Europe: Grandeur and Decline* (London, 1967), p. 137.
18. Taylor, review of *Like It Was*, p. 33.
19. Muggeridge, *Like It Was*, p. 65.
20. Malcolm Muggeridge, *The Green Stick* (London, 1972), p. 263.
21. Heller and Nekrich, p. 195; cf. Ivan Bunin as quoted in the same volume, p. 243.
22. Leonard Schapiro, "Epilogue: Some Reflections on Lenin, Stalin, and Russia," in *Stalinism: Its Impact on Russia and the World*, ed. G. R. Urban (Cambridge, Mass., 1986), p. 424.
23. Anthony Powell, *Faces In My Time* (London, 1980), p. 84.
24. J. R. Kist, ed., *Daumier: Eyewitness of an Epoch* (London, 1976), plate 7.
25. Anatole France, *Le Lys Rouge* (Paris, 1894), chap. 7; *Crainquebille*, iv.

26. Quoted by Robert Conquest in *The Harvest of Sorrow: Soviet Collectivization and the Terror-Famine* (New York, 1986), p. 320.
27. Paul Johnson, *A History of the Modern World from 1917 to the 1980s* (London, 1983), p. 345; cf. pp. 307-8.
28. Conquest, p. 320.
29. Heller and Nekrich, p. 236.
30. Conquest, p. 306.
31. Heller and Nekrich, pp. 236-37.
32. See Conquest, p. 306.
33. Muggeridge, *The Green Stick*, p. 257.
34. Ibid., pp. 257-58.
35. Malcolm Muggeridge, *My Life in Pictures* (New York, 1987), p. 31.
36. Hilton Kramer, "From Russia with Heroism," *New York Times Book Review*, 5 June 1977, pp. 3, 42.

PREFACE

IT would be absurd for me (or for anyone) to attempt to evaluate, at this stage, the Russian Revolution as an episode in the history of Russia and of Europe. There is, of course, Trotsky's vivacious "History of the Russian Revolution," which is really an enormously inflated pamphlet of self-justification, and which, in the most engaging manner, blows the gaff as far as the Soviet régime is concerned, and should, therefore, save discerning readers the expense and weariness of an Intour. There is also M. Rollin's admirable "La Revolution Russe." Apart from these two books I have found nothing amongst the voluminous literature dealing with post-Revolution Russia which attempts more than giving, as the Americans put it, a slant on the Noble, Interesting, Amazing, Portentous Experiment or Racket (according to your slant) at present being carried on under the caption, Dictatorship of the Proletariat. Certainly I have attempted no more myself.

What I mean is that the Russian Revolution is one thing and the Soviet régime another, and that whereas the former is a complicated and, for the moment, insoluble historical problem, the latter is as accessible as, say, the Brain Trust, which, indeed, in many respects it strikingly resembles.

My slant, I must admit, runs racket-wards. I took a

great dislike to the Dictatorship of the Proletariat, and, even more, to its imbecilic foreign admirers. What is more, I found that by following its many tributaries to the main stream, and the main stream to its source, I arrived at something of more general significance that made understandable much that had formerly been incomprehensible to me. In a sense I might almost say that at the ultimate source, at the place where water was bubbling up from the earth, I found myself.

This made describing the Dictatorship of the Proletariat and its works more complicated. I could not just collect and classify stupidities and brutalities. I wanted to bring out their significance as a whole, and in relation to one another; to debunk, not for debunking's own sake, but in such a way that the debunkage would itself have a meaning. Thus I had to be a bit of a novelist as well as a reporter. Thus the episodes in my book are truth imaginatively expressed, and the characters real people imaginatively described. Thus instead of the usual formula—"The characters and events are imaginary, and are not intended to relate to real characters and events"—I would put, "The characters and events are real people and real events (those with a taste for the sport may even amuse themselves by trying to spot the originals); but no particular character or particular event is necessarily real." Whatever others may think of this procedure, it has enabled me to present a faithful picture of what I saw in Russia; and by no other procedure could I have presented as faithful a picture.

The greatest asset of Bolshevik propaganda has been

the naïve, and quite unfounded, belief, held by English people particularly, that it is possible to describe the Soviet régime fairly, and in detachment. They like to think that both sides of the question have been seen; that the describer is a referee rather than a player; that all the pros and cons have been dispassionately weighed. As a matter of fact, of course, in regard to a thing like the Dictatorship of the Proletariat, there are no referees. Only players. And a player masquerading as a referee; accepted by the spectators as a referee, is worth more to his side than the most accomplished player. The vast army of sympathetic critics of the Soviet régime have done more to enhance its prestige than all its paid agitators and subsidised publications put together. By being sympathetic they have accepted its premises; and once the premises are accepted, criticism becomes irrelevant. As a Jew in the Soviet Foreign Office said to me once, with a wink, "Those that are not against us are for us." I quite agreed. It is no more possible to describe the Dictatorship of the Proletariat dispassionately than to describe a mad bull rushing round a field dispassionately. The moment you become dispassionate you automatically make the false assumption that the bull is not mad, and thereby vitiate anything further you may have to say about the matter. Of all the accounts of the Soviet régime that have been written and spoken, the falsest—the ones least related to the facts—are by people who affect to have no prejudices or convictions either way.

I went to Russia in a silly enough mood. All the same, I realised even then that either there was no

Fabian Fairyland; no I.L.Peaches down in Georgia; or the Fairyland was in process of coming to pass under the patronage of the Dictatorship of the Proletariat. Well, it is coming to pass; and the interesting thing about living for a while in Russia is that you find out what it's like, and what the fairies are like. Moreover—oh, rare sight!—you see our own fairies playing and gambolling together for the first time in their lives in a real fairyland; hear their ecstatic shouts and merry laughter; note the happy capers they cut (category A, B, and C travellers) when they find themselves at last amongst their realised dreams and aspirations. I treasure as a blessed memory the spectacle of them going with radiant optimism through a famished countryside; wandering in happy bands about squalid, overcrowded towns; listening with unshakable faith to the fatuous outpourings of obsequious Intourist guides; repeating, like schoolchildren a multiplication table, the bogus statistics and dreary slogans that roll continuously—a dry melancholy wind—over the fairyland's emptiness. There, I used to think, an office-holder in some local branch of the League of Nations Union; there a godly Quaker who once had tea with Gandhi; there an inveigher against the means test and the blasphemy laws; there a staunch upholder of free trade and speech; there a preventer of cruelty to animals; there scarred and worthy veterans of a hundred battles for truth and freedom—all, all chanting the praises of the Dictatorship of the Proletariat. It was as though the Salvation Army had turned out with band and banners in honour of some ferocious tribal deity, or as though the organ of a vegetarian society had issued a passionate plea for cannibalism.

In the classified list of stupidities and brutalities which I did not make, and which is not worth making (stupidities and brutalities, being universal, are neither here nor there), is one item which I have always promised myself the pleasure of stressing if ever I had the occasion. I refer to the position of foreign journalists in Russia, and to the manner in which news about Russia reaches outside. There is a stiff censorship, of course; but it is not generally known that foreign journalists in Moscow work under the perpetual threat of losing their visas, and therefore their jobs. Unless they consent (which most of them do) to limit their news to what they know will not be displeasing to the Dictatorship of the Proletariat, they are subjected to continuous persecution, varying from tiresome reproaches from petty Jewish Foreign Office officials to the imprisonment and exiling of any friends or relatives they may have who are unfortunate enough to be Soviet citizens. The result is that news from Russia is a joke, being either provided by men whom long residence in Moscow has made completely docile, or whose particular relationship with the Dictatorship of the Proletariat puts its words into their mouths, or by men who, while trying to say more than they can, are forced, for interested and quite legitimate reasons, to be discreet. It is even not unusual for agents of the Soviet Government to bring pressure to bear in editorial offices when the correspondent in Moscow is not to its satisfaction; and, so thorough is the Ogpu, I have had to be scrupulously careful, in writing this book, not to introduce any recognisable Russian character unfavourably disposed towards the Soviet régime.

In consequence of all this, the credulous organs of the Left in England are systematically misinformed about Russia, while the credulous organs of the Right, lacking genuine information, make their case against the Dictatorship of the Proletariat absurd by overstatement and invention. A state of affairs, I need scarcely say, that is entirely to the satisfaction of Moscow. So completely successful have these tactics been that now the most preposterous assumptions about, for instance, the success of the Five-Year Plan are made in ordinarily trustworthy quarters; and all let's-see-both-sides-free-trade-free-speech-one-man-one-vote-fairplay-for-India publications are reeds through which the Dictatorship of the Proletariat can whistle what it pleases.

MALCOLM MUGGERIDGE.

February, 1934.

WINTER IN MOSCOW

CHAPTER I
REVOLUTIONARIES

"Dès l'origine, Danton a compris l'objet final et l'effet définitif de la Révolution, c'est a dire la dictature de la minorité violente; au lendemain du 14 juillet, 1789, il a fondé dans son quartier une petite republique indépendante, agressive et dominatrice, centre de faction, asile des enfants perdus, rendez-vous des énergumènes, pandémonium de tous les cerveaux incendiés et de tous les coquins disponible, visionnaires et gens à poigne, harangueurs de gazette ou de carrefour, meurtriers de cabinet ou de place publique." — T<small>AINE</small>

"From the beginning, Danton understood the final object and definitive effect of the Revolution, that is to say, the dictatorship of the violent minority; on the day after 14 July 1789, he founded in his quarter a tiny independent republic, aggressive and arrogant, the center of a faction, shelter for the forlorn, meeting place of fanatics, den of iniquity for all hotheads and for all the available scoundrels, dreamers and reactionaries, muckrakers from the daily papers or street gossipers, murderers from the government or from the market place." — T<small>AINE</small>

CHAPTER I

REVOLUTIONARIES

BILL walked round and round the Red Square. It was late October and the air was cold. He turned up the collar of his overcoat—a little man; face lean and pinched, anxious; step restless; eyes always either angry or sulky, now angry. Above the Kremlin a flag, flood-lit, burnt like a flame. It was blood; and Bill, looking up at it joyfully, drank it in great gulps, humming as he did so the "Internationale":

"Who was nothing shall be all. . . ."

The mighty had been pulled down from their seats and trampled underfoot; and the humble and meek had been exalted. Bill was exalted.

He was a town councillor in Bow, and accustomed to make protests. "Mr. Mayor, I protest. . . ." Here in the Red Square protests were unnecessary. They had been made long ago, and the protestors had inherited the earth.

"I might have been a trade union boss with my thousand a year like so many betrayers of the working class," Bill was fond of saying in the Bow recreation ground, where, every Saturday evening, he addressed open-air meetings. "I might have got into Parliament and had a fat Government job. But I wouldn't do it. Why? Because it would have meant betraying the class I'm proud to belong to."

This thought had eaten at his heart for thirty years. It was the fount of the strident, bitter eloquence he poured out each Saturday evening in Bow recreation ground. Now he saw something infinitely more desirable than a thousand a year or a seat in Parliament. He saw within his reach; felt shoot through his veins, power, naked, absolute, intoxicating; power to destroy; power that like fire would scorch up his enemies and make their world a wilderness.

The fantastic domes and towers of the Kremlin were dark shapes against the sky. Kings had lived there under golden domes, and now Bill. A coloured church like a grotesque dream, irrelevant; unconnected with the earth or the sky or with space, bulged absurdly into the night. It seemed somehow familiar. Had he seen it before? Built it up in his mind when he rained words on to impassive faces spread out beneath him in Bow recreation ground? Was it himself? Denial of everything, yet existing, having substance? "Revolution," he whispered; and his lips twitched, and his eyes grew slightly bloodshot. "Revolution."

Bill wanted to make a speech. He wanted to stand there in the Red Square on a little platform, and, with a printed placard in front of him explaining who he was, express his delight at finding himself at the centre, the very heart, of the first proletarian State that had ever existed in the history of the world. Passers-by were sombre. They did not share his ecstasy. They seemed pale and exhausted and indifferent. Bill scarcely noticed them. He only saw the Kremlin, and the flag burning like a flame above it.

Each time he passed Lenin's tomb he paused for a moment. Soldiers with rifles and fixed bayonets guarded the door. Inside the little man lay in his glass case; a pink head resting on a red cushion; beard carefully trimmed; small hands clenched; finger-nails daintily manicured; materialist conception of history. The pink head embalmed in a vacuum and made immortal, satisfied Bill.

He had come to Russia as leader of a delegation, bringing, as he explained whenever possible, fraternal greetings from the toiling masses in England to the triumphant proletariat of the Soviet Union. "We, representatives of the British working class," he wrote to the *Moscow Tribune*,

> "wish to record our appreciation of the comradely treatment we have everywhere received in the course of our visit to this country to take part in the celebrations in connection with the fifteenth anniversary of the glorious October Revolution. The only criticism we have to offer of conditions here, which give the lie to the cowardly slanders of the capitalist press, is that the state of the lavatories leaves something to be desired. We shall carry back with us to our own country, where capitalism, though decaying, is still dominant, hope and inspiration for carrying on the struggle for a world proletarian revolution."

The editor of the *Moscow Tribune* had added a footnote to the effect that the complaint about lavatories would be transmitted to the Commissariat for Hygiene.

Wind blowing through the clear night from Siberia took the edge off Bill's ardour. He began to feel a little irritated; tried to light his pipe by crouching down into his overcoat; remembered the deplorable condition of the lavatories. They really ought to look after them better, he thought. They're a disgrace.

* * * * *

The same evening Bill was taken to an anniversary reception given by Vox, the Society for Cultural Relations with the Soviet Union. How gay the company was! What a contrast with mayoral receptions in Bow! How informal and comradely!—a band playing; a table loaded with food and drink, and people helping themselves; one man, Bill noticed, filling his pockets; everywhere animated talk, movement. He wished that people abroad who talked about famine in Russia could see this. The Dictatorship of the Proletariat at play. The Dictatorship of the Proletariat unbending and making merry.

Bill sidled up to the table and began to eat.

"My name," a grey-haired American said to him, "is Dr. Canning. You may know, or have heard of, my daughter Beatrice Canning."

She was on the other side of the table; an immense woman, red-cheeked; a kind of passionate stupidity in her eyes, a monumental idiocy.

"My son," Dr. Canning went on, "is a Y.M.C.A. branch secretary; so that both my children in their different ways are serving the Cause."

He looked complacently across at Beatrice.

"Her book, 'Sex and the Soviets,' made a great sensation in the States."

Beatrice was a veteran in the revolutionary struggle. It appeared that Trotsky had once made advances to her in a taxi. He had, she often recounted, rested his historic hand on her knee; and she, perhaps mistakenly, had withdrawn the knee from his grasp. Besides this, she had stood shoulder to shoulder with the toiling masses of Russia for no less than ten years in their struggle to create a classless, socialist society.

"How do you like being back?" she shouted gaily to Claude Mosser, a Jew with a soft, romantic face; somehow a little hard, even shifty, underneath its softness.

"Marvellous," he answered. "How stimulating everything is! How exciting! Admit the faults; but the life, the movement, the exhilaration of it all! A new society going through its birth pangs. A new civilisation."

Beatrice nodded. This kind of thing was her speciality. She hoped Mosser was not going to encroach on her territory.

"I suppose you'll be visiting the old village and the old folks again?" she said, her voice solemn, religious.

Mosser had already written three books about revisiting the old village and the old folks. It was just like Beatrice, he thought, to imagine that a theme was never exhausted. The books had been excellent sellers, certainly; but there was no point in flogging a good horse to death. Besides, ever since it had been suggested, unkindly and quite groundlessly, that the Treaty of Versailles had put his birthplace in Poland he had been touchy about the old village and the old folks.

"This time I'm going to write about industrial construction," he said shortly, and turned away.

"Gleaming roads; the poetry of the machine; music of the siren and hooter," she murmured after him.

There were faces Bill knew; a party of Fabian investigators. They here? he thought; compromisers, Judases, betrayers of the working class. One of them, Mrs. Eardley-Wheatsheaf, was asking questions in her high, quick voice of Mr. Aarons, and noting down his answers in shorthand.

"What happens when the women factory workers have babies?"

"We have State maternity centres," Mr. Aarons answered modestly, gently; his face oval and sallow; faint black beard sprouting round his chin. "They get a month's holiday with pay."

"Full pay?" Mrs. Eardley-Wheatsheaf asked, head on one side like a little sharp bird. No deceiving her. No taking her in with generalities.

"Full pay," Mr. Aarons soothed. "Of course, full pay."

Mrs. Trivet bore down on them; bare pink legs swelling out of tweed skirt; heavy breasts quivering; pale eyes lost in a soft vague face.

"Oh, Mr. Aarons," she said breathlessly, "can you tell me about abortions? They're free, aren't they?"

"Not exactly free," he corrected; always precise; always ready to admit failings where they existed; "but within everyone's means; and, of course, carried out in State hospitals by the most up-to-date methods."

"Do you do foreigners?"

Mr. Aarons looked a little anxious. Her figure was inconclusive.

"There are certain formalities," he said. "If you'd care to visit one of our State abortion centres . . ."

"I should," Mrs. Trivet said rapturously; "tomorrow."

In another part of the room Mr. Trivet looked about him. He was as wizened as his wife was fluid, and had come grudgingly on their tour of investigation, comforted only by the thought that the enlightened Russian proletariat bathed in the nude, and that he might find a comsomolka; slim and ardent; red kerchief round dark hair, who would tell him about her sexual life. His Intourist guide (not, it is true, dressed for the part —silk stockings, smart hat and fur coat; trophies of past category A travellers) might have met his requirements except that Mrs. Trivet shared her with him. He wanted a comsomolka all to himself. There were private, bitter questions he wanted answered before he could decide whether all was well or not with the Dictatorship of the Proletariat.

A bell rang, and an elderly Frenchman in an advanced stage of decomposition began to address the company.

"It's Henri Bernoit," Dr. Canning whispered to Bill. " My daughter Beatrice presented me to him."

Bernoit's decay was venomous, intense. He slobbered out words with senile ferocity. His debilitated body trembled with joy because the mighty had been pulled down from their seats, and because the meek, Bernoit, had inherited the earth.

"I see a vision," he shrieked in vibrant French—hands wildly gesticulating, moisture glistening like dew on his moustache—"of the toiling masses in every corner of the world looking up from their misery, from their degradation, with hope in their eyes because of what you have achieved in your great workers' republic under the mighty Dictatorship of the Proletariat; under the leadership of the Communist party and Comrade Stalin."

He collapsed suddenly into a chair. Someone gave him a glass of vodka, which he drank greedily. There was tumultuous applause.

Mrs. Eardley-Wheatsheaf digested her notes in a corner. It all looked very well, she thought. As a member of the L.C.C. she had often visited public institutions—schools, hospitals, waterworks—but she had never inspected anything that for size and general excellence approached Mr. Aarons's interesting Soviet Union. It was gratifying, too, to find that so many things she believed in had been put into practice—co-education, sex equality, humane slaughterer, family allowances, communal kitchens, all enthusiastically approved by Mr. Aarons, and therefore by the Dictatorship of the Proletariat. Even in the matter of proportional representation, he had explained to her an ingenious arrangement they had for the election of district soviets which, if not proportional representation, was, as he had said, something very like it.

"After all," he had pleaded, "we can't do everything at once. It takes time. Personally, I have no doubt whatever that within the next few years all our elections will be based on proportional representation."

As to the unquestionably repressive nature of the régime, Mrs. Eardley-Wheatsheaf thought that visitors from more civilised countries ought to keep their heads and to see things in proportion. It was true, as she explained at many subsequent lectures, pursing up her lips tightly, perhaps a little venomously, that Soviet officials sometimes disappeared (she accentuated the word "disappeared" to give it its full significance); and naturally she deplored such goings-on, just as she deplored the press censorship and the suppression of all opposition opinion. At the same time she had to admit that, given the peculiar conditions prevailing in Russia, administrative disappearances carried with them certain advantages which she for one was not going to overlook.

How agreeable, she thought, tingling with Bernoit's eloquence, if Alderman Butterfield, who had publicly called her an incompetent, sentimental busybody, could be made to disappear! How agreeable to command his disappearance! How agreeable, instead of writing and talking, to be able to act; to give orders; yes, and to destroy; to purify all the institutions of the State, and, more important, their personnel. Mrs. Eardley-Wheatsheaf's chest swelled under her brown woollen jumper; and her eyes glowed. Like Bernoit she saw, as in a vision, the illimitable possibilities of the Dictatorship of the Proletariat.

Again the bell rang. After having heard Bernoit the company was shown Gorki. Supported on either side by burly members of the Moscow branch of Vox; an ancient sea-lion spouting unintelligible noises; his decay more spiritual, more gentle, than Bernoit's; a kind of surprise, a sense of unreality, a mute appeal for mercy, in his drooping moustache and mouth, he bowed shakily in response to the ovation he received. Then he was taken away; and a telegram from Frank Bernard, the famous Irish poet, was read out:

> "Warmest greetings to Vox on tenth anniversary. In lunatic world Vox represents one of few sane institutions. Despite slanderous campaign of capitalist press truth about Soviet Union being realised abroad. Europe drifting hopelessly and inevitably towards bankruptcy and war looks with growing admiration and fear at triumphant creation of socialist society in Russia. Ideas of New Testament and Fabian essays and Intelligent Child's Guide to Socialism at last being realised. Wish you many more years of useful service."

Bill felt that the moment had come for him to say a word. He stepped forward and cleared his throat preparatory to delivering fraternal greetings. Just as he was about to begin, however, the band struck up again, and everyone moved towards the dancing floor, where, for the first time in Moscow, the rhomba was being danced. The Commissar for Foreign Affairs had learnt it on his last visit to Geneva to attend the Disarmament Conference, and with a beginner's enthusiasm was vigorously shaking his little plump body to its rhythm.

Mr. Trivet soon followed, nervously clasping, as far as it was possible, Beatrice Canning in his arms. She may not be a comsomolka, he thought; she may not be slim and ardent and wear a red kerchief; but at least you can say of her without any qualification that she believes in free love. He looked up at her tenderly and whispered, "I've read your book, Miss Canning. It made a great impression on me. Also I've read articles of yours in the *Moscow Tribune*; and they, too, made a great impression on me. They brought out, if I may say so, the poetry in Soviet life. They made this wonderful experiment seem human and real."

Beatrice, intent on trying to reproduce on the larger scale of her own body the movements that the Commissar for Foreign Affairs was executing in so spirited a manner with his, smiled in appreciation of the compliment.

"Back of the figures; back of the graphs," she said, "there's the insistent urge of youth; passionate; not to be denied. . . ."

"Oh, Miss Canning, is there really?" Mr. Trivet interrupted. "Tell me about that. I want so much to know about that."

Bill's fraternal greetings, though hoarsely delivered, were drowned in the music of the rhomba, and in appreciative comments on the Commissar for Foreign Affair's remarkable performance. Only a hunchback named Taubkin seemed to have noticed his speech.

"Thank you, comrade; thank you," he said. "Try some vodka."

They drank together.

"All these," Taubkin went on, waving his long arms—a great beak of a nose overshadowing his face—"are scum. They don't count."

Bill was gratified.

"The real people keep apart—in the Kremlin; in Lubianka. I only come," he said confidentially, "because of the eats."

Lord Edderton was muttering to himself as he walked up and down. "In coal production the Plan ninety-two per cent. fulfilled. That's an increase on last year of, let me see, twenty million tons a month; or, seventy thousand tons a day, or put another way, five trucks a minute."

He looked round for his interpreter.

"Why do people have to stand in queues for bread?" he asked, his pale blue eyes troubled for a moment. Then, shaking a finger, "Now don't deny that they do, because I saw them myself."

The interpreter smiled. He had been for some years a waiter in a London restaurant; and his clothes even now were somehow like evening dress—butterfly collar and low-cut waistcoat. To answer Lord Edderton's question he bent over him, speaking respectfully into his ear as if to explain away a complaint about the fish.

"Everyone asks that question," he said. "And it's so simple really. Of course the Government could do away with queues; but they don't want to—yet. Don't you see, the workers are so enthusiastic about the Five-Year Plan, and so eager to liquidate illiteracy, that if it wasn't for standing in queues they'd never take any rest."

"You might at least provide seats," Lord Edderton suggested petulantly.

"So we shall in time. Give us time." Then, after a pause; promising a savoury so excellent as to obliterate all memory of the fish. "How would you like to see the War Commissar to-morrow?"

Lord Edderton's face brightened.

"Very much indeed."

"Well, I've arranged it. We're to lunch at the War Office at three o'clock. We'll have to be punctual. Voroshilov's a demon for punctuality. There's a fellow for you!—impulsive, impetuous. You wait till you see him."

Lord Edderton nodded.

"I'd like to see Stalin, too," he said; "but it doesn't seem fair to worry him. He must be so busy."

The reception began to warm up. A Soviet man of letters amused a circle of admirers by sticking plates on his bald head; and Radek, stiff dark bristles outlining his face, ran nervously about like a sly ferret, trying at once to escape from his own deviations and to find an audience. Bill, slightly drunk, sitting by Taubkin, heard fragments of conversation across the table.

"It's a decree of victory, I tell you. They're gettin' away with it again. Gettin' away with murder. Gettin' away with the harvest even if they have to harness peasants to the ploughs. Why not?"

It was Jefferson, a journalist, rapping out his opinions; his face shiny and his eyes alcoholic; two massive, tremulous chins.

"It's always been my viewpoint," Claude Mosser answered, "that the Cossacks deserved to suffer. Look what they did before to the Jews."

He was not going to let this business about the old folks being Poles prevent him from having opinions on the peasant question generally.

The clatter of Jack Wilson's heavy Russian boots broke into their conversation.

"This sort of show makes me sick," he was saying to Fay, a heavily built American Jewess on the staff of the *Moscow Tribune*. "Jesus Christ, what is it? Shop-window dressing. Give me Magnetogorsk. Twenty-four hours' work a day, and more. Peasant boys who couldn't read or write five years ago handling complicated machines. That's the real thing. Jesus Christ, yes."

Fay looked up at him respectfully through horn-rimmed spectacles; a blond giant; very sure of himself; very pleased with himself. Genuine proletarian, she thought; the real stuff; better even than Boris who lived with, and on, her.

"Oh! Mr. Wilson," she said, "I wish you'd take me to Magnetogorsk one day."

"I tell you, sir," an American voice boomed, "that I know a bit about electrical undertakings; and this power-station at Dnieprostroi is a big thing. As I figure it out this whole experiment in the Soviet Union is mighty interesting and mighty important. Yes, sir, a big thing."

In a corner of the room sat Lily Jones, a negress with black curly hair. She had come to Russia with a negro party whose object was to produce a film about the colour problem in the United States. Their enterprise, however, had been brought to an end before it had been properly begun because the Dictatorship of the Proletariat, acting on the advice of one of its American experts, had come to the conclusion that, though a film dealing with the wrongs suffered by coloured races at the hands of capitalist imperialism would edify the toiling masses in Russia, it would be bad for American recognition. Most of the negro party had returned to suffer the wrongs their film was to have ventilated; but Lily Jones had stayed on to study the Russian Revolution, and to make personal contacts in Moscow. Mr. Trivet, eyeing her wistfully, wished that he might make a personal contact with her, but lacked the courage to penetrate the circle of admirers packed closely round her.

One of these admirers seemed to Mr. Trivet particularly formidable—an officer in uniform; tall and rubicund; perpetually smiling.

"Who is it?" he asked Mr. Aarons.

"Our *chef-du-protocol*," Mr. Aarons answered, and went on to explain with a certain pride how M. Flerinski had been in the Tzarist diplomatic service, and how he was now a convinced Marxist and a member of the Communist party. "He's a link," he said gaily, "between the old régime and the new. We have such links. You mustn't think (shaking a finger) that all the old aristocrats are against us, or (smiling) that we've shot them all."

Mr. Trivet did not much like the look of M. Flerinski. As a link between two régimes, he thought, he reflects credit on neither. There was something flabby and revolting about his rubicund amiability. The sort of man, Mr. Trivet thought, who follows you about in Marseilles trying to persuade you to go to a dirty cinema. The sort of man . . .

"Geoffrey," Mrs. Trivet shouted to him, "this is wonderful. I must write it all down at once. Come, Geoffrey. A memorable evening."

At two o'clock Lily Jones was sitting between the director of the press department and his immediate predecessor in that office. The one, Ouspenski, was short and dapper, with gold teeth and layers of curly hair; the other, Mikhailov, was florid and plump, with grey hair brushed smoothly back from his forehead. Each with an arm round her waist, the two Jews fenced together across Lily's body.

Mikhailov said that it was a great relief to him to get away from the trivial routine of the press department, and to be in the provinces actually at grips with the problems of socialist construction.

Ouspenski retorted that, as a student of human nature, and as a man with a diplomatic career in front of him, he found his work in the Foreign Office fascinating.

Mikhailov said that it was only by using all his influence with the Government, and by talking personally with Stalin, that he was able to get transferred from the press department, where, rightly or wrongly, he had been regarded as indispensable.

Ouspenski retorted that when he was appointed to his present post it was made clear that he was to consider it only as a stepping-stone to something much more important.

"What sort of socialist construction do you do?" Lily interrupted.

"At the moment," he answered, "I'm director of the State Bank at Stalingrad."

"Isn't that marvellous!" she answered. "Isn't that just too marvellous!"

"Of course," he went on, "I take a great interest in the output and efficiency of the factories; and then I give lectures to shock-workers, and sometimes I take a hand myself at the bench or at excavating."

"You do?" Lily said. "Well, isn't that just marvellous! Now I'm collecting material for some short biographies of the great Soviet leaders. You don't happen to know any new anecdotes about Lenin, do you?"

Her two companions shook their heads as though to say, "No, but we know a lot of good anecdotes about Ouspenski and Mikhailov."

"You've heard, I take it," Ouspenski said, "that I recruited and led a company of Cossack cavalry in the Civil War."

Lily looked serious.

"I suppose you know," Mikhailov said, "that I was wounded in Amsterdam when an attempt was made to assassinate my chief. Fortunately I was able to receive in my shoulder the bullet that was intended for his heart."

He opened his double-breasted blue coat and showed a small revolver outlined in one of the pockets of his waistcoat.

"Since then I never go unarmed."

Ouspenski was quite ready to leave Mikhailov with the last word. He had Lily's cloakroom ticket in his pocket; and that was worth any number of revolvers.

"You must tell me some more anecdotes," Lily said to Mikhailov as Ouspenski led her away, "and then I'll include you in my biographies."

Mikhailov said that he was ready to tell her any number of anecdotes any time.

All the caviar had been eaten; all the bottles had been emptied; even the Commissar for Foreign Affairs had tired of the rhomba and gone home to bed. Bill and Taubkin picked their way amongst the debris of Vox's tenth anniversary. Jefferson's voice still resounded through the room; more solemn now; more mellow; words tending to run into one another.

"Gettinaway with things. Gettinaway with murder. Gettinaway with the harvest. Gettinaway with everything just as they always have and will. Big country. Big, big country. Lots of people. Millionsanmillions of people. What's it matter a few millions more or less?"

"Thank you, Mr. Jefferson," Mrs. Eardley-Wheatsheaf said, shutting up her notebook. "I wanted very much to get your point of view. Very interesting. Good-night."

She put her notebook in her pocket. No one had her cloakroom ticket.

*   *   *   *   *

Bill and Taubkin walked along deserted streets; unsteadily and arm-in-arm.

"Scum," Taubkin muttered. "Amount to nothing—Aarons, Mikhailov, Flerinski, Ouspenski, Commissars. What are they? Just clerks. My clerks. Our clerks."

They went downstairs to an underground café; and Taubkin ordered beer and dried salt herring. Bill seemed to remember having read something about beer and dried salt herring in a book by Maurice Dobb; Marxist study group for working men; shrivelled lady from the London School of Economics reading to them in her high-pitched, dry voice:

> "Should the visitor to Russia leave the automobile or droshky and chew dried salt herring and sip beer while he listens to the fiddler playing wild gipsy songs of the steppes in a small *peevnaya*, he can hardly fail to sense that here there is something important and new . . . absence of cap-touching . . . certain confident bearing amongst working men and women . . . new social equality . . . divorced from a worship and evaluation of success in money terms and from deference to the man who has won a financial position above his fellows and shows it in his habits and dress and bearing."

The band struck up a jazz tune; and a boy in a mauve suit with wide trousers and a tight coat did a step dance. The couples fox-trotted; rather clumsily except for the pro; dressed in plus-fours and a grey woollen jumper over one of whose pockets the word "cricket" was embroidered. Bill found the atmosphere more congenial than Vox's anniversary celebrations. It was more like a Bow public-house; more like the French

Revolution as he had seen it on the pictures; more proletarian.

"These are workers," he said appreciatively, "and not just clerks."

Taubkin laughed. He was always either vehement or cynical. When he spoke his face either darkened with passion or broke into hundreds of amused wrinkles.

"Workers with beer five roubles a bottle and bread a rouble a slice," he jeered. "They're mostly criminals and speculators; otherwise they wouldn't be able to be here."

A girl with bleached hair and bright lips leant over Bill. "English," she whispered. "Valuta."

The word seemed to pass from mouth to mouth. It seemed to electrify the place. "Valuta! Valuta!" echoed and re-echoed through the smoky, pungent cellar. Fox-trotting couples paused in their dancing. A man sleeping with his head on a table looked up to find out what was the matter. Bill was frightened.

"What's happened?" he asked.

"Foreign currency," Taubkin answered, excited like the others. "Dollars, pounds, francs, marks. Have you got any? They buy real food. Butter, sugar, meat." Then, repenting: "Let's get out of here quick."

Again Bill was walking round and round the Red Square, this time with Taubkin. The Kremlin was in darkness now, and the Square empty except for the soldiers guarding Lenin's tomb; the still night colder than ever; the long winter ahead like a shadow over Moscow. Many shadows over Moscow. Terror and famine and death. Bill saw no shadows. He still looked up at the flood-lit flag.

"The real people," Taubkin said, pointing to the Kremlin, "are here."

He was a little wistful, and regretful that he had forgotten himself in the underground café.

"When I was in Tennessee working for the I.W.W.," he went on, "they tarred and feathered me; in the night, carrying torches, and laughing because I looked so funny tarred and feathered with my hump back and my big nose."

He became exalted. He waved his long arms in the air. His voice was bitter, like the screech of a bird swooping down on to a lake to kill.

"This is my revenge."

Bill understood what he meant, and did not need, therefore, to ask him on whom he was being revenged.

* * * * *

Mr. Aarons turned on the wireless before going to bed. He sat listening to it in his study—books neatly arranged; complete works of Lenin; Marx in black limp leather; gramophone with records in a case at the side; oil paintings of Engels and Marx and Lenin and Stalin on the walls; photograph album with snapshots of himself and his wife on holiday at Blankenburg neatly pasted in it.

His admiration for the Dictatorship of the Proletariat was quieter, less passionate, than Taubkin's. After all, he thought, remembering his conversations with Mrs. Eardley-Wheatsheaf, Mrs. Trivet and Lord

Edderton that evening, we've got an unanswerable case. He built up the case once more in his mind, and leant back satisfied; one formula leaning against another; the whole frail structure standing because his hand was sure and careful, and because he held his breath.

Turbulence had deposited Mr. Aarons safe and sound amongst oil paintings of Engels and Marx and Lenin and Stalin; and he looked back on it as a seaside visitor looks down from a pink promenade on waves lashing against rocks. Turbulence belonged to the past; and it only remained now to see that every Soviet home had its wireless, and its gramophone, and its shelves of revolutionary literature, and its portraits of revolutionary leaders. That would come in due course. Meanwhile, as a beginning, Mr. Aarons had them.

Moments of uncertainty troubled him sometimes. He was by nature mild and gentle; and the excesses of the Dictatorship of the Proletariat brought doubts into his mind. Yes, Mr. Aarons doubted. Was it quite clear? Was it altogether reasonable? Violence and intolerance and cruelty; things repellent to him, seemed much in evidence. A promising young curate marked out for preferment, he faltered sometimes as he mounted the pulpit steps; brooding on the Thirty-Nine Articles, on apostolic succession, on the virgin birth; coughed and stuttered; then, miraculously, a formula expanded, engulfed foreign matter; and the sermon proceeded without hindrance.

Mrs. Aarons, wearing a long white nightgown, her

hair in five tight plaits, looked in on him. Her voice was sharp and discontented.

"Well!" she said. "Well!"

There was no pink promenade from which to look down on this turbulence. Shrinking, he waited for the waves to break over his head. They broke.

* * * * *

The next day the streets of Moscow were illuminated. Everywhere red streamers decorated with revolutionary slogans; soaring graphs; figures that mounted to dizzier and dizzier heights; cardboard battleships and motor-cars; printed placards marking where new hotels and skyscrapers were to be built; busts of Lenin and Stalin; silhouettes of Marx and Engels and Lenin and Stalin shading into one another like Jesus sitting in the lap of Mary and Mary in the lap of Anne. It made the city more than usually fanciful and unreal. The dreams and aspirations of the Dictatorship of the Proletariat took tangible shape in terms of limelight and pasteboard. An enormous multiple store fitted with the apparatus of salesmanship but with nothing to sell; an election campaign without any candidates; impersonal, abstract festivities keeping alive an idea, as Lenin was preserved in his glass case, by creating a vacuum round it.

Dark masses of people strolled amongst these slogans and graphs and figures and cardboard motor-cars and busts, staring at them; quite silent; their faces expressionless; like a river flowing through an empty lighted town. They were the proletariat. For them it had all happened. They were the multiple store and its stock;

buyers and what was bought; election campaign and candidates; idea and the vacuum that preserved it; proletariat and Dictatorship of the Proletariat. Fifteen years before they had risen up and destroyed. What could they destroy now? Only themselves. And when they had destroyed themselves, what remained? It was, perhaps, an unconscious awareness of this impasse which made their processing through the streets so funereal; like Pharaohs inspecting the trappings of their own tombs.

Bill, walking to the Opera House, was not at all funereal. Limelight and cardboard satisfied him as Lenin's embalmed head had satisfied him. He found them gay and hopeful. Their unreality pleased him; made a heaven with many mansions; was the pomp and circumstance of his and Taubkin's revenge. Come unto me all ye who travail and are heavy laden and I will revenge you. As Mrs. Eardley-Wheatsheaf continually pointed out, it was a new religion.

The Opera House glistened like a jewel. Mrs. Trivet hastily scribbled down for use later in a book, "A Woman Writer Amongst the Soviets," that she intended to write:

> "Workers in coloured blouses rubbed shoulders with Red soldiers and important Communist officials; apple-cheeked peasant women with gay shawls over their shoulders or heads were sitting side by side with earnest-looking students who read while they waited for the meeting to begin; Mongols with high cheek bones, Orientals from Turkestan, Esquimaux from Northern Siberia . . ."

She looked round to see if there were any Esquimaux, and, finding none, decided to take their presence on trust.

"Cossacks from the Kouban—all were there; all eager and animated; some of the younger people obviously lovers; delightfully unaffected and unselfconscious in the simple caresses they exchanged—pressure of the hand; arms round one another; even, in one case I noticed, a kiss. What a pleasing contrast with the kind of thing that goes on in our cinemas! The Embassy folk in their evening clothes looked curiously remote, out of things; even, I thought, a little absurd. No one, however, took any notice of them."

There was a blast of music, and the curtain rose, revealing an enormous wheel round which was written, "Physical Culture." Slowly, majestically, the wheel began to turn; and, at the same moment, light flooded the back of the stage where a massive bust of Lenin draped in red stood out against a background of factory chimneys, arranged to form a hammer and sickle, and belching real smoke which wrote across a crimson sky, "Dnieprostroi is finished." Massed round the base of Lenin's bust were Soviet athletes who, when the orchestra struck up, took their places on either side of the wheel, shouting as they did so, "Hurrah for the Five-Year Plan completed under the leadership of the Communist party and Comrade Stalin in four and a quarter years." Limelight played on them; lusty young men and women, scantily clad, and powdered and rouged; women with shaven armpits. Mr. Trivet looked enviously at his neighbour, who had opera glasses. I must tell them about this in Bow, Bill thought. "May it not be," Mrs. Eardley-Wheatsheaf remembered to have read somewhere, "that Russia will evolve a new attitude towards the human body; more like the Greek than the Christian; not, perhaps, idealising physical beauty as such; seeking rather health and efficiency and strength; none-the-less, doing away with all sense of shame in the feelings of men and women about their bodies?"

The back of the stage darkened again; and the great wheel, still moving, glowed internally. Coloured lights flashed on to the faces of the athletes. The men were wielding imaginary hammers; their muscles straining as they built enormous factories; sweat glistening on their backs and foreheads. The women were shooting with imaginary rifles; alert; active; some of them lying down and some kneeling; all intent on destroying the class enemy and defending the Dictatorship of the Proletariat. Imperceptibly, the music to whose rhythm they moved, changed. Bill knew the tune. He began to hum the words under his breath:

> "If you were the only girl in the world
> And I was the only boy . . ."

himself piling socialist brick on socialist brick; destroying enemy after enemy, as he hummed. The back of the stage was once more illuminated; the great wheel turned more and more furiously. Socialism was built, and the class enemy utterly destroyed. To the singing of the "Internationale" the curtain fell.

When it rose again a long table covered with a red

cloth had been placed in the centre of the stage. From the back of the theatre came the sound of marching feet. First appeared from either side a file of six cyclists wheeling their bicycles; then a file of six soldiers wearing gas masks; then two dispatch riders on real motor-cycles; then six airmen in smart blue uniforms each with a pair of golden wings on his breast. At the same moment a party of marines let off a furious volley of machine-gun fire from the foot of Lenin's bust; and Voroshilov rode impetuously on to the stage on a live horse.

"I had lunch with him today," Lord Edderton whispered to Mrs. Trivet.

The machine-gun fire ceased. Soldiers, airmen, and marines all stood stiffly to attention. From what had once been the Imperial boxes trumpeters sounded a flourish; and the Dictatorship of the Proletariat filed in and took their places at the long table. Everyone applauded. Lord Edderton was beside himself, and waved a red handkerchief in the air. Even Mrs. Eardley-Wheatsheaf, who seldom gave way to her feelings, was seen to rise from her place with her eyes glistening. As for Mrs. Trivet, she longed to get back to her hotel and write it all down. It would make, she thought, a whole chapter in "A Woman Novelist Amongst the Soviets."

Bill looked curiously at the Dictatorship of the Proletariat. He wanted to identify himself with it. He wanted to feel that it was himself. His heart went out in adoration of the Dictatorship of the Proletariat, and inwardly he chanted his Magnificat:

"He hath showed strength with his arm;
He hath scattered the proud in the imagination of their hearts.
He hath put down the mighty from their seats;
And hath exalted the humble and meek."

What men! he thought. What men!

"Lord, now lettest thou thy servant depart in peace."

His eyes filled with tears; and his face softened; and he forgot at last that he might have been a trade union boss with his thousand a year. He was reverent.

Stalin sat in the centre of the long table; sombre, unintelligent, possessed with energy; dark hair growing low on his forehead, and small dark eyes set closely together; gloomy and lonely and barbarous and Asiatic; more impressive on the whole than the pink head in its glass case; more morbid; more powerful. The pink head, after all, might have bobbed about quite happily in parliamentary lobbies and committee rooms; on government and opposition benches. It might, after all, have been an honourable, or even right honourable, pink head. Stalin was different. He had never chattered away evenings in dingy lodgings, or spent indigestive afternoons playing chess in cafés in Paris or Vienna, or loitered, a proletarian rentier or remittance man, by the Lake of Geneva. He could become, and remain, the Dictatorship of the Proletariat because he so utterly hated and despised the proletariat. Product of a Jesuit seminary; home-bred Napoleon content with domestic conquests; class-war Napoleon; pogrom Napoleon, he had the sense to see that the only purpose of the Revolution was to make someone—Bill, Mrs. Eardley-Wheatsheaf, Mr. Aarons, Lord Edderton—Tzar, and, seeing this, to make himself Tzar.

The rest of the Dictatorship of the Proletariat was shadowy enough; mediocrities capable of flattering and of effacing themselves; echoes more or less distinct; a curious company, ghostly, unreal; spending their days together in the Kremlin; reading newspapers they had written long ago, written and forgotten; seeing everywhere their own portraits and busts, and hearing everywhere applause; half believing and half afraid; utterly apart, not only from the world in general, but from Russia, from Moscow; they too embalmed, preserved in a vacuum; dim, superannuated tyrants with memories of old victories and enthusiasms, and fears for the future; anxious tyrants whose very arrogance was thin and apprehensive; shadows filling an empty space where the Dictatorship of the Proletariat was supposed to be.

Molotov, one of them, delivered a speech. His fat soft cheeks bulged out on either side of a microphone. Without any gesture, his voice quite even except when, every now and again, it broke into a frenzy of stuttering, he orated. His stuttering made the microphone kick and splutter like a motor-car with dirt in its carburettor. Statistics trailed off into inarticulate noises.

"We have built up heavy industry, and equipped our collective farms with the most up-to-date machinery. This year we produced in our own factories and from our own material . . ."

His face grew anxious and pained. He dreaded the struggle that he knew was coming.

"Five hundred and twenty-eight hun hun hun hun hun . . ."

In a frenzied effort to deliver the statistics he shook his ponderous head from side to side.

"Hundred thou thou thou thou thou . . ."

Then, abandoning the struggle and shouting defiantly:

"Tractors."

Applause was orderly but noisy, as though each member of the audience was trying to convince himself and the others that he entirely approved of what had been said. The audience applauded in the same way that schoolboys laugh at a headmaster's jokes.

The next speech was by an old Bolshevik, who explained how in the past he had been guilty of deviations; how he had supported opposition movements, and how, to his everlasting shame, he had admired, and even been friendly with deviators now justly expelled from the party and exiled.

"My only regret," he said, "is that they haven't been shot as they deserved."

As he spoke he swayed gently backwards and forwards as though he was slightly drunk; slobbering his repentance into the dictaphone; hanging over it like a sentimental commercial traveller over a barmaid.

"Hypocrite! Insincere!" someone shouted.

The shout was taken up. It seemed the right thing to do to shout "Hypocrite! Insincere!" It seemed the Party Line. The flow of repentance was checked, and the penitent turned from his microphone and faced the Dictatorship of the Proletariat.

"Perhaps I am insincere," he said in a changed voice; quieter but more penetrating. "It's not easy to be enthusiastic about a speech of this kind."

There was silence. Someone had said what he meant. Someone had spoken. It was terrible. The cardboard became cardboard, and the limelight, limelight. The athletes and the soldiers and marines were painted clowns, and the Dictatorship of the Proletariat vain old men grouped round a maniac. The great wheel, glowing internally, was a silly pasteboard wheel. The enormous bust of Lenin was clumsy and grotesque. Someone had spoken. Someone had dared to speak. The audience suddenly remembered Russia and what it had become. How long? they asked themselves. How long? and were afraid.

Stalin frowned; and the penitent returned to his microphone, and poured his repentance into it with more zeal than before.

*   *   *   *   *

Bill's moment came when he unfurled the banner that he had brought with him from England, and, with his delegation behind him, joined the procession that was to march across the Red Square. It was a cold day, and windy. The wind played with the banners, and denunciations of capitalism and imperialism, and cardboard figures that the procession held up to the sky.

This was the proletariat honouring itself. The stream of people that had flowed in rivulets through the streets of Moscow the evening before was canalised now into one great slow-moving river emptying into the Red Square; faces floating on its surface, and banners poking out of it, and swaying like reeds in the wind. It floated past Mrs. Eardley-Wheatsheaf and the Trivets and Lord Edderton; past Vox massed round Gorki and Bernoit; past Mr. Aarons moving gently from one spectator's bench to another; past the *chef-du-protocol* smiling amongst diplomats; past Jack Wilson and Fay; past Ouspenski and Mikhailov, each holding one of Lily Jones's arms; past Lenin's tomb, on a ledge of which stood the Dictatorship of the Proletariat. A slow-moving muddy river with faces floating on its surface and banners swaying like reeds in the wind, it washed round the Dictatorship of the Proletariat.

Songs and slogans sounded faintly, being drowned in the rattle of tanks and armoured cars; the marching of infantry and the clatter of cavalry; the buzz of aeroplanes in the sky. Stalin stood a little in front of the others; Napoleonic; a hand over his heart. Come unto me all ye who travail and are heavy-laden, and I will revenge you. It was the only reality. The rest was nothing.

* * * * *

Jefferson, a whisky and soda at his elbow, typed:

> "fifteenth anniversary of october revolution celebrated today with impressive military display and great popular enthusiasm stop molotovs stirring yesterdays speech stressed five year plans achievements which inconceivable except under proletarian dictatorship stop urged renewed efforts for

outcarrying soviets great purpose dash creation classless socialist society stop eye been present ten october revolution celebrations but none as impressive and enthusiastic as todays stop under banner second five year plan soviet unquestionably ongoing industrialisation policy and awaygetting with it. . . ."

CHAPTER II
PROLETARIAN MYSTICISM

"Que l'on donne à ces grands professeurs modernes la possibilité pleine et entière d'abolir la vieille societé pour la reconstruire à nouveau, il en résultera de telles ténèbres, un tel chaos, quelque chose de si grossier, de si aveugle et de si inhumain que tout l'édifice croulera sous les maledictions de l'humanité, avant même qu'il soit achevé de construire." — DOSTOYEVSKY

"If these great modern professors are given the full and utter possibility of abolishing the old society in order to reconstruct it anew, it will result in such gloom, in such chaos, something so gross, so blind, and so inhuman that every building will collapse under the curses of humanity, even before they have a chance to finish construction." — DOSTOYEVSKY

CHAPTER II

PROLETARIAN MYSTICISM

THE class war hung over the North Caucasus and over its population like a heavy cloud; filling the fields with weeds; killing off cattle and horses, and spreading famine and trouble everywhere. Under the direction of the Ogpu the Red Army ravaged the country. Hundreds of thousands of peasants were exiled, and thousands shot. Everything edible except some millet and potatoes was requisitioned by the Government. These potatoes were counted over one by one like jewels.

It was steppe country, stretching endlessly into the distance; like a desert only it was populated and scented with fertility. The loneliness of the desert was tempered by a sense of things growing, and the curious emotions; the hopelessness and despair and resignation, that are called up by an enormous expanse of country or of water, softened because of the little Cossack villages dotted about everywhere. Moonlight, making trees dark shadows and streams a silver network, filled the place with a kind of troubled peace. It was between Europe and Asia; neither orderly nor indolent; now a battlefield of the class war.

One evening in late November when an icy wind that had been blowing for days dropped suddenly, and there was a pause, warm and still, in expectation of the winter's first snowfall, a party of six soldiers with an officer entered a farmhouse some little distance from a market town. The house was silent and dark. There seemed to be neither people nor cattle. The officer had a torch, which he used to find his way about, and which darted here and there like a little restless moon. Once he shouted angrily, but there was no reply. Once he struck his head against a beam, and swore. A room in the farmhouse was warm. It smelt of human life. The light of the torch, feeling into the darkness, illuminated two eyes, a face, pressed against the wall.

"Let's have some light," the officer, Comrade Babel, said. A peasant woman lit a lamp.

The room was scantily furnished. There were wooden chairs and a table; on the wall an ikon garlanded with coloured paper chains, and two wedding groups. An old man was sleeping on the stove, and three children sitting against it. The woman who had lit the lamp had a curious face; young-looking, although her hair was grey and her skin wrinkled; oval and plump in outline, yet actually haggard; angry and defiant, but its immediate expression frightened. She seemed to be two people in one.

Comrade Babel sat down at the table, and the soldiers stood about carelessly with their rifles. He was half Italian, but had lived in Russia for many years; eyes and eyebrows sharply tilted; projecting cheekbones and smooth black hair making his face look like a white triangle crossed by a thin line, his mouth. It was a cruel, coldly fanatical face. The woman and he looked at one another. They were class enemies.

He took some papers out of his pocket; and she stood waiting for him to speak.

"I see," he said, "that your taxes are in arrears, and that you've only delivered a third of your grain quota."

"You took away my husband."

"A kulak."

"Where is he?" she asked, suddenly passionate. "Where have you taken him? Is he still alive?"

Comrade Babel shrugged. There was a pause. He lit a cigarette; then, looking up quickly, asked, "How much grain have you got hidden?"

She had expected the question, and answered stolidly, "You took everything before."

"The usual answer," he said.

"Can't you see," she went on, pointing to her children, "that we're starving? We haven't any of us tasted bread for weeks."

"Yesterday," he said coldly, "five hundred poods of grain were found that had been hidden in the ground by a woman whose children were swollen."

She began to sob; and the children, taking their cue from her, sobbed too. Only the old man on the stove, her father, slept on untroubled.

Comrade Babel ordered the soldiers to search the house thoroughly. Their heavy boots clattered up and down wooden stairs. They pulled up floor boards, and opened cupboards, and searched amongst the rafters and down in the cellar, but found no food anywhere.

"These people bury grain," Comrade Babel said. "They've always done it." Then, turning to the woman, "We'll come tomorrow in the daylight."

While he was speaking one of the soldiers—a Mongol, face leaden and smooth like a ball except where two little slit eyes and two little nostrils and a little mouth punctured it—went over to the old man on the stove and playfully stirred him. Noticing that the top of the stove stretched farther than he had thought, he reached over, and, feeling about, gave a shout. Behind where the old man was lying was a sack of flour.

When the soldiers returned to their quarters in the market town one of them was carrying the sack of flour, and another marching the old man along at the end of a rifle. No one who saw them was surprised. It was a common enough sight at that time.

* * * * *

The woman sat down to think. What was to happen to her? She and the children were starving, and alone. She remembered the little procession lined up in military formation on a railway station platform in the very early morning before it was properly light, and with a thin rain falling; her husband and perhaps nineteen others, all carrying bundles, guarded by soldiers; the last she saw of him. She remembered fifteen years before a crowd round a burning house; herself in the crowd, and full of joy because the flames leaping up into the sky meant that she was to have land that she could keep for ever. She remembered her husband pushing home a barrow loaded with things he had stolen; a silver vase; a heavy plush curtain; a uniform coat; odds and ends he had picked up when they looted the house before setting fire to it.

She remembered civil war; one army after another sweeping over the country; all rapacious; all needing food. She had given food and starved without losing hope. It was a matter of indifference to her which army won and which lost as long as she could feel round her, like a body round a soul, earth that she owned. She remembered meetings by Lenin's statue, that stood outside the church in the village square, and resolutions and pledges and acclamations. These, too, had not touched her.

Now it was different. Suffering and privation had become meaningless. She felt that her life had been torn up by the roots, and made insignificant. She hated the Dictatorship of the Proletariat because she recognised in it a force determined to destroy her. A ruthless, irresistible force. Something against which she was helpless. Between her and the Dictatorship of the Proletariat there was the class war.

The children had fallen asleep. There was nothing to give them when they awoke. No food, and no hope of getting food. The sack of flour that she had hoarded so carefully and used so sparingly had been taken away. She went into an outhouse and fetched an axe, a little rusty from disuse, but still in fairly good condition. Her fingers felt along the edge of the axe, testing it; then, with well-directed strokes, she killed her three children one after the other, doing the job so skilfully that none of them awoke or uttered a cry. She tied each of the children up in a sack, and carried the sacks and the axe upstairs, and hid them amongst the rafters.

Snow was just beginning to fall when she set out for the market town. It came down gently in thin flakes, and brushed against her cheeks. Tall weeds reminded her of the class war. She felt the desolation it had brought to the country—a kind of blight; a kind of organised sterility; paralysing human beings and making the soil barren. This autumn with no harvest stored away and no hope in the spring that would follow was to her not a season but an end, a death. Walking through the unreality of a first snowfall, having murdered her three children and hidden them in sacks in a loft, it seemed to her that nothing had substance; that she was dead too; the earth itself; everything.

When she reached the market town she made her way to a house with green shutters, newly painted, and after some difficulty got herself admitted to Comrade Babel's presence. He was sitting over the litter of a meal; his pale face slightly flushed, and a slight unsteadiness about his speech and movements. Opposite him sat his wife; a blond, plump and soft; lips and cheeks heavily rouged; long, coloured finger-nails. The high collar of his uniform jacket was unfastened.

"Well?" he asked, irritated at being disturbed.

The woman explained how, after his visit, she had thought things over and had come to the conclusion that on the whole it would be better for her not to try any longer to defy the Dictatorship of the Proletariat; how she had three sacks of grain hidden away which she was prepared to deliver up if he would come and receive them; how she realised at last that her own and the country's best interests would be served if she joined a collective farm, and how she intended to take that step the very next day.

He was not eager to leave his warm room and go out again in the snow; but she pleaded with particular intensity that she might be allowed to disclose her hidden store of grain without delay, and to him personally. She even went down on her knees; wept; abased herself; and at last he yielded. Perhaps it flattered him to think that a woman noted for her defiant attitude should refuse to make her final surrender except to him. Perhaps, with a view to later searches, he was curious to see where she had hidden her grain.

"These Caucasian peasants are cunning," he often used to say; "but one's cunning is like another's. When you know them it's easy enough to see through their tricks." Perhaps, despite her weeping and abasement, he read a challenge in her eyes; and, being an officer on the class war front, felt bound to take it up.

Walking back with her along the road; quite white now; covered with new snow that deadened their footsteps; three soldiers behind them, he felt afraid. After his warm room the cold dazed him and made his head swim. He felt himself to be alone and surrounded with enemies. An unreasoning panic possessed him. Neither his fanaticism nor his sense of duty was strong enough at that moment to prevent him from realising the rôle he played—a destroyer; a flaming sword; vengeance for remote sins; servant of remote ideals. How they hate me! he thought; and it seemed to him that hate rose like a mist from all the villages he had visited; blinding him; choking him. My hate against theirs, he thought. The class war.

"The children," the woman said aimlessly, when they reached the house, "are in bed."

Comrade Babel nodded. He wanted the business settled quickly, and to get home again.

"Where is it?" he asked.

"I'll show you," she said. "Bring your torch. It's dark in the loft."

In the loft! he thought. They were supposed to have searched the loft. He was eager to know where the grain was hidden. Each of these farmhouses had a loft.

The three soldiers did not know whether they were expected to follow upstairs. They delayed, talking for some reason in whispers. Perhaps they were afraid of being cursed for not having found the grain when they searched the loft earlier in the evening. Or perhaps they had a feeling that this phase of the class war was between her and him, and that they had no part in it.

It was, as the woman had said, dark in the loft; and Comrade Babel shone his torch. He had thought that the soldiers would follow, and wanted to call them, but was too proud, or found his lips too dry to shout.

"Over here," she whispered. "Over here," and led him towards the rafters. He saw three bulging sacks. Fools! he thought, to have missed them. I sometimes think they're in league with the peasants. Tomorrow I'll look into the matter. She felt about for the axe where she had hidden it, and brought it down on his head. Unlike the children, a dry soft cry came from him as he fell forward.

She went downstairs. "You can go and fetch the sacks now," she said to the soldiers, and waited, triumphant, for them to bring down her three children and the man she had killed. She heard them floundering about in the darkness of the loft, their heavy boots shaking the floorboards. Then one of them shouted. They came running down, expecting her to have fled; surprised to see her still standing there and waiting for them. They stared at her stupidly, not knowing what to do.

"The sacks?" she asked eagerly. "Where are the sacks?"

"You killed him," one of the soldiers said.

She nodded. They did not love Comrade Babel; but still, to have killed him like that! We'd better take her back, and the body, and the sacks, they agreed amongst themselves.

* * * * *

The affair was reported in Moscow. An Ogpu officer had been murdered. It was serious. Comrade Babel's comrades stood for two minutes in silence mourning him—casualty on the class war front; faithful servant of the Dictatorship of the Proletariat murdered while carrying out his duties; one more martyr. Babel's body lay a-mouldering in the grave, but they went marching on. Who next? they asked themselves, and thought, Work in the villages is getting more and more dangerous. They used the term "work in the villages" with the same intonation and in the same sense that missionaries do.

Bolshevism, like an enormous stomach, threw out digestive juices and assimilated the affair. It was translated into correct Marxist terminology. The complex mind of Bolshevism; dark, and full, like a ghetto, of narrow tortuous streets; full of unexpected turnings and blind alleys, worked on the affair until it became sanctified. Against black velvet curtains, and with the orchestra softly playing the Song of the Volga Boatmen, Comrade Babel in golden armour was treacherously slain by a green dragon. Was it conceivable that the dragon had acted alone? There must be a plot. Enemies were once more holding up their heads; and unless drastic action was taken Good would be destroyed by Evil. Yet another morality play must be staged to safeguard and fortify the Dictatorship of the Proletariat.

Pravda published a leading article headed, "We must increase class vigilance on the agricultural front":

> "Unless we root out mercilessly all hostile elements in the villages our socialist economy is in danger of being wrecked. The Five-Year Plan, triumphantly completed under the leadership of Comrade Stalin in four-and-a-quarter years; the envy and the despair of the capitalist governments of the world, has equipped us for heavy industry; now all the mighty forces of the Dictatorship of the Proletariat must be massed on the agricultural front for the spring sowing campaign. Traitors must be put out of the Party; our blows must fall with increasing severity on opportunists; class enemies must be made to feel the full force of our revolutionary laws; the class watchfulness of the

PROLETARIAN MYSTICISM   63

courts and procurers must be intensified. An enemy outside the Party, let it be remembered, is less dangerous than an enemy inside the Party...."

* * * * *

In a high gilded room in the Kremlin, once the Tzar's bathroom, Kokoshkin looked over a report:

> "The woman, wife of an exiled kulak; herself a notorious counter-revolutionary, lured Comrade Babel to her house with false promises.... Murdered him in the loft with an axe.... Three soldiers waiting downstairs suspected of complicity... Symptomatic of new tactics of kulak elements.... Apparent submission used as a cloak for sabotage and other treasonable activities.... Work sometimes from within collective farms; sometimes even from within Party organisations. .... New propagandist campaign and sterner measures against class enemies needed to root out this evil."

He was a Jew; formerly a shoemaker; almost bald, and with a beard trimmed like Lenin's.

As he lay in his bath he brooded on the report; soft limbs, white and hairy, relaxed in hot water; red pate glowing in a mist of steam; little eyes half closed. Enemies at work everywhere; secret underground enemies, corroding the Dictatorship of the Proletariat; enemies in the Party, perhaps even in the Polit-Bureau; enemies all round him night and day, intriguing, sabotaging. After all, he knew the ways of secret underground enemies since he had been one himself; since he had cobbled away in the sunshine on a bench outside his little shop in Kiev with a printing press hidden in his cellar, and at night had printed leaflets that were passed from hand to hand in the factories; since he had decayed a social order from within until it fell like ripe fruit in his lap.

The class war has reached a new phase, he thought, as he dried himself. A critical phase. We must destroy our enemies until not one is left. Only then shall we be safe.

That evening he had to address a conference of collective farm shock-workers. Words poured out of him easily as he thought of the woman with her axe in a dark loft waiting for Comrade Babel.

"They come to you now," he orated, "with soft words. Do not listen to them. They lure you to destruction by pretending to be your friends. Do not trust them. The kulak has changed his tactics. He can no longer be recognised by his vile face and his red neck and his harsh voice. He speaks fairly. He is gentle and sweet; a holy man. You all know what happened to Comrade Babel; how he was lured to his death with friendly words; how he paid with his life for having trusted an enemy. Learn from his fate and beware."

A great wave of feeling swept him along. The ingratitude of it! The pity of it. Oh! the pity of it!

"We have done everything for them, and they answer our kindness with hate. We have saved them from landlordism and usury, and, instead of gratitude, we get stabs in the back."

His Jewish religious heart swelled; and his eyes filled with tears.

"But their plots will be unavailing. Already our achievements are great. They will in the future be greater still. By drawing the entire mass of poor peasants into collective farms we have succeeded in raising them up to the standard of middle peasants. This is a great achievement; such an achievement as not a single state in the world has ever before secured."

Now he was triumphant, prophetic; mouthpiece of the Lord of Hosts; very Lord of Hosts.

"Comrade Babel must be numbered amongst our blessed dead; but we, the living, will see to it that his death shall not have been in vain."

* * * * *

Foreign journalists were waiting in the Foreign Office for the text of Kokoshkin's speech to be given to them. They walked up and down a corridor, or sat over their typewriters in a red plush room. Some had secretaries; smart girls; Sonya, Tanya, Nadya. Cooley, an American, looked pale and anxious. He was always afraid that Hartshorn would get a beat on him.

"Looks like being a swell story," he said to Hartshorn, trying to hide the tremble in his voice.

He had an uneasy feeling that Hartshorn understood things better than he did. Understanding things had always been a difficulty with him.

Hartshorn nodded in a non-committal way. "Yeah," he said, "looks like being a swell story."

Cooley wanted to be friendly. It was, he felt, a moment when co-operation was to his advantage. He decided to offer a week-old discovery on the altar of friendship.

"Did you happen on Krupskaya's article on fairy stories? Very interesting and very significant. Her viewpoint was that the time had now come when some of the old traditional Russian fairy stories should again be told to Soviet children. As I figure it out this means that the censorship generally is going to be relaxed. She instanced Goldilocks, so I took that as my lead. Goldilocks reinstated. Five hundred words. Do you think I overfiled?"

Ouspenski appeared, bland, smiling, and distributed the text of Kokoshkin's speech. The secretaries translated in undertones, without emotion and without punctuation; and Cooley listened eagerly. With luck it might hit the front page. An ex-President of the United States had died, and there was his funeral that day. Even so, if he gave a good lead, they might find room for it.

"Sending much?" he shouted to Hartshorn, who was already typing.

Hartshorn nodded without looking up.

Cooley closed his eyes and saw headlines. They flashed across his brain in letters of fire. Living words. Words that became flesh; tasty; appetising; salacious:

"BOLSHEVIK LEADER'S FIGHTING SPEECH."

"KULAKS LIKE HOLY MEN."

"KREMLIN DISCLOSES AGRICULTURAL PLANS."

"KOKOSHKIN FACES THE PEASANTS."

The last, he thought, was the best, and began:

> "kokoshkin red dictator stalins chief lieutenant faces peasants stop bolshevik leader in fighting speech urged collective farm shock-workers intensify . . ."

Jefferson sat in a corner by himself. He was an old hand and needed no translator. Sometimes he looked rather tired and wistful. So many fighting speeches since he'd been in Russia. So many leads and declarations and conferences. So many thousands and thousands of words typed and then telegraphed. He was half sick of visions, and at times thought of clearing out; perhaps even taking Sonya with him; then settling down in New York on what he'd got saved in the bank, and trying to write stories. *Saturday Evening Post.* Once you got the trick it was easy enough. Easier even than sending messages from Moscow. Only there was no security. Not even money in the bank was security. Not even money in several banks and in several currencies. He loved New York; smart people; really smart people who weren't getting away with it but had got away with it; a little flat in a tall block, fitted with labour-saving devices, and a cocktail bar, and shaded lights, where he could bring a girl after a show, and lounge about, and make love in a straightforward American way. Here there's no comfort; no security, he thought bitterly, and skimmed through Kokoshkin's speech.

The structure and the sentiments were familiar. It was scarcely necessary to read it before beginning to type:

> "last night addressing collective farm shock-workers kokoshkin stressed necessity ruthlessly crushing opposition kulak elements to governments collectivisation policy stop bolsheviks determined harmonise agricultural economy with industrial development plan stop admittedly involves cruelty and casualties like other forms war but dash putting it brutally dash impossible make omelettes uncracking eggs . . ."

One by one the typewriters stopped. Cooley was the last to finish. He read over what he had written. It was a front-page message. It had to be a front-page message. He set his jaw; head Germanic with a bull neck and a white slow face; easily perspiring; little beads of sweat now on his forehead. A front-page message:

> "in historic hall formerly scene tzarist splendour now legislative chamber peasants hailing all parts soviet union assembled and attentively listened kokoshkin dash bearded orientals moslem women late harem . . ."

Hartshorn, he thought complacently, wouldn't have bothered about the Tzarist splendour and the Moslem women; and he hoped that he might get a complimentary telegram the next day—"great stuff—keep it up"—to reward him for his pains.

Ouspenski read over their telegrams, and signed them with a flourish, occasionally altering a word here and there; nothing much because the messages were inoffensive. Kokoshkin's eloquence made quite a good showing. Digested, vomited, redigested, revomited, it made a tasty fragment of news to be consumed during breakfast between one cup of coffee and another; eye on the clock because a train to catch; anxious as to whether bowels would stir; still able to understand from an arrangement of letters and of type that Kokoshkin had faced the peasants.

* * * * *

Later, their work done, the foreign journalists assembled in the bar of the Metropole Hotel, where they could get the drinks they liked, and pay for them in dollars, and dance with their smart wives far into the night. Mrs. Cooley; exquisitely preserved; slim, with curling eyelashes and belladonna eyes; no back to her dress; her mouth an unchanging red curve, whispered to Mrs. Hartshorn; very like her, only the plan executed on a larger scale, as the last course of supper was served, "The trouble about Moscow, dear, is that one always overeats."

"All the same," Mrs. Hartshorn answered, "it's very interesting."

It was a swell bar with a cocktail mixer in a white coat, and might have been in New York or Berlin or Paris.

* * * * *

In the North Caucasus the night was clear and frosty; rolling country, white against the black night, and the stars so near that they seemed to mix with the clusters of lights marking where villages lay; above each village the dark outline of a bulbous church. Winter had set in, and the peasants hid from the class war on their stoves, and tried to sleep through as much of the day as they could because asleep they forgot that they were hungry.

The woman who had murdered Comrade Babel with her axe was shot. Her body was tossed aside like something unclean; her life stamped out by the Dictatorship of the Proletariat; all trace of her obliterated. She had been an enemy, and now was removed. As Mrs. Eardley-Wheatsheaf (now busily engaged in arranging the material she had collected; preparing broadcast talks, lectures, articles, a book) would have put it, she disappeared. She was dead wood; something that had to be cleared away. Her death had been planned long before. It occurred in a logical, an inevitable, sequence of events. She was the past; and Bill and Taubkin and Mrs. Eardley-Wheatsheaf and the Dictatorship of the Proletariat had abolished the past. An idea flashing like lightning through space struck her down. As Jefferson (now drinking whisky and soda, and wondering who he knew on the staff of the *Saturday Evening Post*) would have put it, she was an egg that had to be cracked before an omelette could be made. As Mr. Aarons (now spending a quiet evening with Mrs. Aarons and the radio) would have put it, she represented a new phase in the class struggle. As Kokoshkin would have put it, her death was one more glorious victory won by a triumphant Dictatorship of the Proletariat.

*   *   *   *   *

The dead bodies of Comrade Babel and the peasant

woman, rotting underground, sprouted and produced a rank crop; hate and fear and suspicion, that was harvested by the Dictatorship of the Proletariat. In Kokoshkin's mind, a ferment; little bubbles stirring, and engendering thoughts and words that sped along corridors and telegraph wires, and collected in typewriters and roll-top desks, and in separate minds; at last in a collective mind. Action followed; swift movement by night; searches; a tearing open of mattresses and a turning over of papers; motor-cars coming and going; long interrogations in rooms so silent and remote that they seemed just space.

When the process was completed, and the crop garnered, *Pravda* announced:

> "Recently the Ogpu discovered a counter-revolutionary organisation in certain departments of the Commissariat for Agriculture, and in certain State farms, especially in the North Caucasus, the Ukraine and White Russia. Most of the officials concerned were ex-bourgeois and White Guard elements. Seventy arrests have been made. A majority of the arrested persons have confessed to being guilty of destroying tractors and agricultural machinery; of setting fire to machine-tractor-stations; of injecting horses with poison bacillus; of speculating with grain belonging to the State, and of destroying live-stock. Their object was to undermine our socialist economy, and to spread famine in the country."

"As I thought," Kokoshkin said to one of his secretaries. "Just as I thought."

Mr. Aarons, going over an abortion centre with a

party of foreign visitors, remarked, "You see the sort of difficulties we have to reckon with."

"We do see," they answered sympathetically, too interested in the abortion centre to follow very carefully what he was talking about.

In a cell in Lubianka prison Professor Tchounikine, formerly of the Moscow Veterinary Institute, was being cross-examined about his part in the counter-revolutionary organisation. He was a little fussy man with untidy hair and blue misty eyes that were absurdly magnified by the thick lenses of his spectacles.

"You prepared this bacillus, and in considerable quantities?" one of his two interrogators asked.

"Yes."

"What for?"

"I was conducting experiments into the possibility of inoculating horses against the disease I'm accused of having deliberately spread."

"And you sent specimens of the bacillus to Kiev and to Rostov and to Kharkov?"

"The veterinary institutes there were collaborating in the experiments."

"Miliukov, for instance, was collaborating?"

"Yes, I think so."

"You think so?"

"I'm sure he was."

There was a pause. The other interrogator came forward like a fresh polo pony.

"Miliukov confessed last night to having injected horses with the bacillus with the object of killing them. Here's his confession. Read it."

Tchounikine took the confession and read it through.

"I had no knowledge of what he was doing," he whispered.

"You wrote to Miliukov last June, just when horses were dying off in hundreds, that the experiment looked like being a great success."

"They died for lack of fodder. I reported again and again. You can see for yourself . . ."

"Miliukov says in his confession that he was acting on your orders."

"It's a lie."

The little man became hysterical. His shrill voice echoed through the cell.

"A lie! A lie!"

He seemed to have been answering questions for days and months. There was nothing in life except questions. There was nothing in the world except space, and eyes staring at him; coming and going; all the same; and cold voices eating like knives into his flesh. Sometimes he fell asleep, and his dreams were full of questions. Were they dreams? Was he asleep or awake? What had he said? What written down and signed?

Once, lying on his bed; perhaps asleep; perhaps awake, he saw a shadow in his cell, and shrieked out, "Who is it?" He knew the voice that answered.

"Miliukov, they say you've confessed. We were friends, Miliukov. We've worked together, and known each other for many years. I read something you'd signed. It wasn't true. Tell them it wasn't true."

He got up to embrace Miliukov, and found himself

sitting back to back with him, and listening to him as he spoke in a curious unreal voice.

"You sent me the bacillus. We'd agreed beforehand to inject horses with it so that the collective farms would fail, and famine turn the people against the Government. We wanted to prepare for a counter-revolution and another intervention. We were an organisation in league with other officials who destroyed tractors and agricultural machinery, and set fire to Machine-tractor-stations. We knew that all this was going on, and encouraged it. We have been guilty of espionage, sabotage, treason, and deserve to be punished."

"You must be mad," Tchounikine said, and found that Miliukov had gone.

A doubt began to trouble him. Had they arrested his daughter? Was she there in the prison, being questioned and tortured as he was? He said her name over and over until he seemed to hear her voice; distant shrieks; appeals to him for mercy. He alone could save her. Had they told him this? He was not sure. Would they bring her in to accuse him as they had Miliukov?

"May I know how my daughter is?" he asked his interrogators once; not people; only eyes into which he stared. They made no answer. Their silence was terrible.

Another doubt. Was he, after all, guilty? Were they right and he wrong? Had he joined a conspiracy to overthrow the Dictatorship of the Proletariat? Had he always been as careful about the bacillus as he should have been? Half hoped that mistakes might be made? Dropped hints to Miliukov and others that if things went wrong it might be for the best?

His spirit broke suddenly. "I confess," he said in the same hard unreal voice with which Miliukov had spoken, and found himself sitting in front of a sheet of paper and writing:

> "I confess that I prepared large quantities of a dangerous bacillus, and dispatched it to other members of the counter-revolutionary organisation to which I belonged with orders to inject horses on State and collective farms so that they would die. Our object was to undermine Soviet agricultural economy; spread famine, and prepare the way for another intervention and a counter-revolution. I knew that other officials were destroying machinery and setting fire to machine-tractor-stations, and actively encouraged them. I confess that I am a class enemy, and that I have been guilty of treasonable activities; and I ask for mercy, knowing that I deserve to suffer the extreme penalty."

The words came to him of themselves, as though they were being whispered in his ear.

"The names?" he was urged. "The names of the other members of the organisation?"

"No," he shouted; himself for a moment. "No names"; then, relapsing, he wrote a list of names at the end of the confession; signed it, and fell asleep.

*   *   *   *   *

He slept, it seemed to him, until he found himself

in a court being tried. It was a large crowded hall, decorated with red streamers on which slogans were printed; at one end a raised table where the judges sat; beneath the table a row of lawyers. He and the other prisoners, Miliukov amongst them, were on a platform. Something was making his eyes blink. He looked up, and saw that limelight was beating on his face. The world's a stage, he thought; reader of Shakespeare; bourgeois antecedents; class enemy. A heaviness in the atmosphere; something sickly, reminded him of theatres he had visited as a student. The same shabby brilliance of light and colour. The same smell of rapt stale people. Hero and villain mouthing extravagance, and the audience morbidly feasting on Good and Evil burlesqued to be equally revolting. This is my body; eat this, he remembered; once religious. Flavour of crowded Easter masses when ikons glared out of incense smoke, and long-haired priests chanted, and candle flames flickered, and little bells rang, and a kneeling congregation groaned and sobbed as it drank blood and ate flesh. Remembered, too, newspapers expectantly unfolded; curiosity with tentacles uplifted creeping after its victim; black and white photographs and newsprint gorged in trains and over hurried meals.

Someone read out the indictment; and witnesses were called. Tchounikine watched the web being made; noted occasional botches; how the thin threads were woven into one another to make the required pattern. He looked down at the audience; a few faces he knew; mostly strangers—Mr. Aarons with his flock;

Cooley gleaning copy; Mrs. Cooley staring curiously at him with her belladonna eyes; at the back workers' delegations with banners and emblems; Bill proudly holding up a piece of cardboard with "Marat" printed on it.

The Public Prosecutor's oratory worked towards a frenzy. His shaven head glistened with moisture; mouth turning and curving like a fungus in the whiteness of his face; little close eyes misty and bloodshot.

"Sabotage," he shouted. "They're all guilty of sabotage. They've confessed to being guilty of sabotage. Everywhere, all round us, sabotage is taking place. I see it in factories, in collective farms, amongst officials, from the highest to the lowest. I see it even in tram-cars and restaurants. Are we to tolerate this?"

The workers' delegations, waiting for the lead, roared "No."

"Then we must destroy our enemies. We must punish, and punish with . . ."

A great answering shout: "Death!"

The word echoed and re-echoed through the hall. It filled the hall. The Public Prosecutor, a slight froth at the corners of his mouth, listened complacently to the chorus he had awakened.

We ought to make some sort of protest, Tchounikine thought. We ought not to lend ourselves to this.

"Mr. President, I protest against the manner in which the court is being conducted . . ."

It would have been in keeping with his life to have thus protested. Turning over the pages of revolutionary literature, and agitating for the Duma to be assembled, and for women to have the vote, and for education to be free and universal, he had dreamed of such protests. Now there was more to protest against.

"Mr. President, as a civilised European . . ."

Civilisation itself seemed flimsy in that hall, and with that word echoing and re-echoing through it; a fanciful pantomime; scene following scene as century followed century. What did it mean to be a civilised European? His eye caught Cooley's. Cooley civilised and ravening after headlines; Cooley civilised and, like the Public Prosecutor, seeing sabotage everywhere; blaring on a front page instead of in a court; awakening choruses in forty million readers instead of in drilled delegations with their banners and their emblems; their "Workers of the World Unite" and their "Marat."

After all, Tchounikine thought bitterly, there's no protest to be made. I've nothing to say. Cooley or the Public Prosecutor—it doesn't matter. Suddenly he lost control of himself and stood up, making absurd movements with his hands.

"All the vilest qualities in human beings," he shouted incoherently, struggling against a slight impediment in his speech; "all that is most dark, most subterranean in human nature; beneath the animal; beneath greed and lust and hate; beneath every kind of appetite; the lowest, darkest depths . . ."

Then, breaking off, he said in a quiet voice: "I withdraw my confession. I am innocent. I wish I had been guilty." Someone was whispering to him. He could not quite catch. The next witness? He should have remembered. Of course, the next witness was his daughter. She would testify against him. After all, he was guilty. A class enemy. A traitor. He began to recite his confession in a monotonous voice. "I confess that I prepared large quantities of a dangerous bacillus . . ."

The court breathed again. His outburst had reminded them of their own precarious situation. They trembled even while enjoying the spectacle of others being gorged. Trembled and wondered. Who else is rank? Who next must be let blood.

Mr. Aarons, mopping his brow (it was hot in the court), said to his flock, "It seems so unfair when our prisoners confess to pretend they're not guilty. Yet (shaking his head) that's what your newspapers do."

His flock agreed with him that it was unfair.

"Anyway," Mrs. Trivet said, "you can rely on us to tell the truth when we get home."

Mr. Aarons smiled gratefully at her.

* * * * *

A man sat in a room in Moscow playing a concertina. He was generally thought to be slightly mad. Children played and howled in the room; and women quarrelled and did housekeeping; but he seemed not to notice them, and just went on pushing his concertina in and out as though he was quite alone. The noise of it sometimes got on people's nerves.

"What's the matter with you?" I asked him once. "Why don't you ever do anything except play your concertina?" When he talked he didn't stop playing, but played very gently. His tunes were indefinite, and ran into one another. It looked as though the music was a drug that he needed. Most people thought that if he ever stopped playing something terrible would happen. That was why no one grumbled about the noise.

"Do what?" he asked.

"Work," I said. "Take some exercise. Join in things."

"I played a part in the Revolution," he answered vaguely.

He struck me as being rather a slow-witted person; the sort of man who reacts slowly, but on occasion intensely; unimaginative, but for that very reason liable to be shaken to pieces.

"We made the Revolution," he went on. "It happened. There was Lenin in power. Shall I ever forget the first Congress of the Soviets when we made our declarations and passed our resolutions? Shall I ever forget the feeling I had that the world was beginning again? We found ourselves on our feet and singing the 'Internationale.'"

He began to play it, but fantastically; introducing extra trills and flourishes into the tune, and making it sound shrill and absurd instead of lugubrious.

"Yes," he said, shouting against the noise of his own playing; "it was a glorious time. I saw a future. All through the civil war and the famine it was the same. What did war and famine matter if the future was open and hopeful instead of closed?"

His shirt bulged open; and I saw his hairy chest

underneath. He was dirty and unkempt; finger-nails uncut; blond irregular beard; yellow teeth; eyes bloodshot.

"I was one of the Kronstadt sailors whom Trotsky called the pride and the glory of the Revolution," he said. "Then I fought in the Red Army. Then I was ordered to shoot down my old Kronstadt comrades. Why?"

He stopped playing the "Internationale"; threw his concertina with a bang on the floor, and stood up; eyes blazing; horror in his face.

"Because they demanded free elections and a secret ballot; liberty of speech and of the press; the right to form trade unions; the liberation of political prisoners; the equalisation of food rations. . . ."

He was telling the points over one by one on his fingers like a child repeating a lesson; monotonous emphasis on each; the drone of innumerable committees; political consciousness of the masses; government of the proletariat by the proletariat for the proletariat.

"Of course," he went on, sensing my mood, "their demands were nothing in themselves. Meaningless. Valueless. I know that quite well. All the same, they were what we had the Revolution for. They happened to be the slogans we'd had on our lips when we died and killed and destroyed. It seemed absurd, after destroying so much to make a place for them, to destroy them too. I wondered what would be left after they'd been destroyed. Now I know."

"What?"

"Nothing!" His voice rose angrily. "Nothing. An emptiness." The women, doing their housework in the room, were frightened.

"He'll get himself into trouble and us as well," one of them said. "Why can't he speak quietly and play his concertina? If he wasn't my brother-in-law I'd complain about him myself and have him sent away."

She picked up the concertina and put it in his hands. He sat down and began to play it.

"It's the only battle I've ever run away from," he mumbled. "Running away from the Kronstadt revolt I met the Cheka running back. Not Russians. Jews and Letts and Poles who'd been frightened when the trouble first started, and now were running back to get their teeth into the pride and the glory of the Revolution." He spat and played a mournful tune; a sentimental dirge; trivial, mean music that made his despair seem trivial and mean.

"Free elections and a secret ballot; liberty of speech and of the press; the right to form trade unions; the liberation of political prisoners; the equalisation of food rations," he told off again on his fingers; then, picking up his concertina, his voice merged in its wail.

"If it all happened again?" I asked.

He made no answer, and seemed to have forgotten I was there.

The women in the room obviously wanted me to go.

"If anyone heard him!" one of them said, and crossed herself piously.

Afterwards I was haunted by the thought of the Cheka racing back to be revenged on the Kronstadt sailors. I saw them like fiery monsters rising out of slime; little eyes flaming; mouths frothing; teeth gnashing as they raced through the night. Dark shadows made up of the fear and hate and fury and envy that hid in the soul of Mr. Aarons, of Kokoshkin, of Mrs. Eardley-Wheatsheaf, of Stalin, of Bill, of myself. Symbols of the new religion Mrs. Trivet described to a sympathetic clergyman friend. Proletarian mysticism.

* * * * *

The monsters sometimes went after smaller game than the pride and the glory of the Revolution. Anna Mikhailova, a teacher, lived in her own little corner without interfering with anyone. She had an ancient edition of the "Forsyte Saga," and a book on architecture, and an ikon beneath which in summer she sometimes put a bunch of flowers that she'd picked in the country. Years of vegetarianism had dried up her skin. She pecked little morsels of food secretly when no one was looking, and had views on education. This secret, furtive life had made the texture of her body disgusting. It had wrinkled and faded like old newspapers stored in an attic. She was fond of animals, and had a particular voice that she used when she spoke of little children; and she believed that languages should be taught by the direct method, and that co-education was a very good thing.

"I am not," she often used to say, "against the Revolution."

In fact, she had in the earlier stages been for it because she had thought that through its agency women would be emancipated (she had wanted to be emancipated), and many good causes find their consummation. Even now, like Cooley, she felt hopeful about the reinstatement of Goldilocks.

When the monsters opened their jaws she trembled, but with great courage said to the three members of the Ogpu who visited her in her room, " I am afraid of mice but not of you." One of them was a Jew with a small dark face; one a blond Esthonian, and one a Russian. They stared suspiciously at her ikon, and asked her searching questions about her class antecedents. The Jew, she thought, looked funny in uniform. She told them that she had been a governess before the Revolution, and that she had lost her papers.

Certain of her pupils, it appeared, had complained that her teaching tended to be romantic. The ikon seemed to bear out the charge.

" Are you a practising Christian?" the Jew asked.

She said she was.

He nodded significantly and made a note.

" My religion," she said, " is my own affair."

" As a person, yes; as a teacher, no," he answered.

The Esthonian read from a paper in a husky voice, " On February 28 you used the phrase, ' Beauty is truth; truth, beauty.'"

" It was a quotation," she said, " from a poet."

" I don't care," he answered. " It's opposed to correct Marxist thinking, and is not allowed. In any case it's nonsense."

She turned to the Russian. "What is correct Marxist thinking?"

He was eager to reply at length, but the Jew interrupted, "Read Lenin instead of bourgeois poets and you'll understand."

She decided not to press the point. On the whole, she thought, I've held my own fairly well.

They were not quite sure what action they had better take. Her room was small, and on the cold side of the house; and her life altogether was so small and contemptible that it scarcely seemed worth bothering about. Was it conceivable, they asked themselves, that such a creature could influence students? Her miserable indeterminate idealism would seem as bloodless and futile as herself. She was a good advertisement of its idiocy.

"You realise," the Jew said, "that from now on you will be under observation, and that any further complaints will have serious consequences."

When they had gone Anna Mikhailova went for a walk. It was a grey, cold, heavy afternoon. Am I under observation? she wondered, and looked round anxiously, excitedly, to see if she was being followed. It gave her a new feeling of self-importance to think that a man might have to follow her wherever she went. Like a virgin about to be raped, she dreaded and thrilled at the possibility of such an intrusion on her solitude.

No one was following her. She walked up and down a boulevard where children played and lonely men and women sat about. Everything was cheerless, hungry; patient queues waiting outside bakers' shops; tram-cars, overflowing with passengers, processing by. If I really gave up my indeterminate idealism, she thought, what would be left? She felt the cold. It seemed to reach to her soul. Shivering, she went home again.

The monsters cracked their jaws over her head and then left her in peace because she was too like them to make a meal. She, too, belonged to darkness. She, too, burrowed underground amongst dry phantoms; general ideas; slave utopias built in grey space; mysticism like fire drying her up; a flaming sword that she plunged into herself instead of, like them, scattering her enemies with it. (They, however, must plunge it at last into themselves.) Being their sister, she was spared.

CHAPTER III
HEAVY INDUSTRY

"Rien de plus dangereux qu'une idée générale dans des cerveaux étroits et vides; comme ils sont vides, elle n'y recontre aucun savoir qui lui fasse obstacle; comme ils sont étroits, elle ne tarde pas à les occuper tout entiers. Dès lors ils ne s'appartiennent plus, ils sont maîtrisés par elle; elle agit en eux, et par eux; au sens propre du mot, l'homme est possédé." — TAINE

"Nothing is more dangerous than a general idea in narrow and empty minds; since they are empty, it would not encounter any knowledge that would be an obstacle to it; since they are narrow, it does not linger to occupy them totally. Consequently, they are no longer their own master. They are mastered by it; it acts in them, and by them; in the proper sense of the word, man is possessed." — TAINE

CHAPTER III
HEAVY INDUSTRY

A TRAIN composed entirely of special sleepers ambled gently from Moscow to Kharkov. It carried a cargo of foreign journalists and distinguished visitors to see the ceremonial opening of the Dnieprostroi hydro-electric station; largest hydro-electric station in the world; triumph of the Dictatorship of the Proletariat and of the Five-Year Plan. Ouspenski was in charge of the expedition. He wore for the occasion a cap with ear-flaps, and plus-fours, and an overcoat with an astrakhan collar; Cooley, leather breeches and a check shirt; Mrs. Cooley, a Hollywood riding habit; and Mr. Aarons, a seedy, old-fashioned bicycling suit and short gaiters. Old Muskett, his beard as luxuriant as Karl Marx's, had on his habitual top-boots and velveteen jacket, and a young man connected with the I.L.P. shorts and a rucksack. They were, as Mrs. Trivet said to Lord Edderton, a mixed and interesting company.

The temperature of the train was kept up; and the restaurant car was generously stocked. Someone had brought a gramophone which played in the short intervals between one meal and another. At the stations peasants collected in wistful groups to stare at such magnificence; and occasionally one of the more soft-hearted amongst the journalists would toss them a piece of bread or a leg of chicken which they gobbled up voraciously on the spot. This, however, as Ouspenski carefully explained, was unnecessary, "Because," he said, "they've got plenty to eat unless, of course, they're kulaks." From inside the heated train the company, replete, looked out at the rolling Ukraine.

Ferdinand Stoope, on a flying visit to Russia to write a series of articles for an American newspaper, chatted enthusiastically with everyone. He was blond and boyish and ardent; a recognised authority on European affairs, and a journalist with a reputation for originality and sprightly writing. Cooley watched him carefully. There, he thought, is a man who's likely to have something up his sleeve. There's a man to keep an eye on.

"I'll be slipping off for a few hours at Kharkov," Stoope said casually.

"You will?" Cooley answered as casually. "Taking a look round, I suppose?"

Stoope nodded, and moved on to get Jefferson's viewpoint on the food situation.

"Tell me about it," he said to Jefferson; his blue eyes full of serious enquiry; his voice earnest. "I want to know about it."

"Of course there's a shortage in some districts," Jefferson said in a tone of emphatic finality. "No one denies that. You might even call it in certain very rare case a famine. But, as I said in a piece I sent a few days ago, you can't make omelettes without cracking eggs."

"You sure can't," Stoope agreed enthusiastically. "I like that phrase. No omelettes without cracking eggs. Very illuminating. Thank you."

He bowed and moved on to collect someone else's viewpoint on something else.

The young man in shorts who was connected with the I.L.P., and whose name was Roden, stared moodily out of the window. He was troubled with conscientious scruples. In the quiet correctness and prosperity of his Quaker home the case had seemed unanswerable. As stated in the *New Leader* it had seemed unanswerable.

"The Ogpu worries me a bit," he said to Carver, a Russian Jew who, like Mosser, had re-emigrated from America to join the old folks.

"I've seen hundreds like you go down one after the other," Carver answered gloomily. "You need strong nerves and a hard heart to get on in this place."

"It seems to be a very powerful organisation, and very much in evidence," Roden went on. "I found a little girl crying the other day . . ."

"You can't tell me anything about it," Carver interrupted. "I'm an authority on the subject." Then, lowering his voice so that Mr. Aarons, who was gently patrolling up and down the corridor, should not overhear, he whispered, "I've served three years for espionage myself."

Roden's general attitude became more respectful; and there was a new note of awe in his voice as he asked, "Was it very terrible?"

The other pursed up his lips and nodded solemnly.

"Very terrible," he whispered, more softly than ever. "Very terrible indeed."

This revelation made Roden's conscience more uneasy than ever. Underneath his small black moustache his lips trembled. After making so many sacrifices for his principles, going to prison as a conscientious objector, renouncing an inheritance, he faced with dismay the possibility of having to undertake spiritual exercises even in Russia.

"Other motives than greed as the mainspring of action. Nobler ideals to fight for than country or empire. (Not that I advocate violence in any circumstances. I mean fight in the sense of striving after; seeking earnestly to attain.) New standards of value. A new relationship between man and man. These are the most notable achievements of our comrades in the Soviet Union." Thus he had spoken at I.L.P. Summer Schools. Now he wondered—a scout-master fearful that blowing bugles might promote a militarist spirit; an ordinand uneasy about the oath he must take.

He sought out Muskett, who was drinking beer at the expense of the Dictatorship of the Proletariat in the restaurant car. Muskett'll comfort me, he thought. Muskett's a veteran. He'll have been through the stage I'm going through now, and'll be able to help. Muskett'll understand.

"Being actually in Russia," he said by way of a conversational opening, "drives one back to first principles, doesn't it?"

Muskett's voice took some little time to find its way through the overhanging growth of his beard. When it emerged it was pompous and damp like a clergyman orating at Hyde Park Corner on a foggy November evening. He was an old decayed tree trunk, outwardly sound and bulky, but soft and rotten inside.

"You need," he said, "to understand this country, inspiration and judgment. I've got plenty of inspiration but no judgment. Jefferson's got both. I've never known him wrong about anything. I always say to youngsters like yourself, a bit bewildered, a bit uncertain, Take him for your guide and you won't make any serious mistakes."

The old man embodied in himself the character of his age. He was the decadence of European civilisation getting a last sensation out of the establishment of Asiatic barbarism in Russia. Lines on his face traced out a record of the world to which he belonged. Coeducation in creases round his nose. Votes for women wrinkling his forehead. Pacifism the slobber of his lips. His faint eyes dimly alight with the afterglow of forgotten irrelevant causes, and his cheeks wearing in an alcoholic flush the passion and enthusiasm, now spent, that had stirred him and his generation; the whole bloated, inflated, but with no core. Though unkempt thoughts, grey and aimless like his beard, still grew in his mind; though the trunk was still massive, it would soon fall and be a heap of putrefying softness. Meanwhile it stood, a melancholy hulk, in the Dictatorship of the Proletariat's vineyard.

Roden felt encouraged by the thought of Muskett's ten years of faith.

"You've seen it all, haven't you?" he asked anxiously. "You know about the Ogpu, and about Carver being sent to Siberia, and about the little girl who was crying . . ."

"Don't make the mistake," Muskett interrupted,

indicating at the same time to the waiter that he wanted another bottle of beer, "of fastening on to details. Keep in mind the main objective. Lenin said once that he never dared to show the lists he received from the Cheka to Lunacharsky because his nerves weren't strong. Ah! Lenin."

His voice softened and became tender.

"Do you know what one of my girl students said to me when he died?—'It's so terrible to think he's gone, because one could take all one's troubles to him.' His death was a sad loss. A sad loss."

Jefferson joined them, and Muskett introduced Roden. "He's a newcomer," he said chuckling, "and has got a bad attack of Ogpuitis. They all go through it. I told him to watch you and he'd be all right."

Jefferson leant back in his chair. "You must see the thing as a whole," he said. "The broad outline. My point of view is very simple. I hate money and I hate sex. That is to say, exploited sex. Marriage. Prostitution. Therefore, I'm happy here."

He was a parliamentary candidate canvassing voters. Vote for Jefferson and no more money or sex.

"Besides," reverting to his favourite subject, "it's a big country."

* * * * *

The train rattled on through the snow-covered Ukraine. It was getting late. In Karl Keightan's compartment a game of poker was in progress. Karl, the most faithful and painstaking admirer of the Dictatorship of the Proletariat, was winning. His heavy face sparkled, and his deep emotional voice, American but enriched by a thick and vacuous earnestness, kept up a running commentary on the game. All the players unbent. Stoope gave up collecting viewpoints, and even Cooley forgot his front page for a little while. Mr. Aarons looked in from the corridor. He would have liked to have joined in the game. Gambling was one of his few weaknesses; but, apart from the fact that they were playing for dollars and he had only roubles of uncertain value, he felt that in view of his position it would be unbecoming for him to take a hand. He watched intently; sharing the players' ups and downs; trembling with them when they were indecisive, and nerving himself to take risks when they took risks, until Mrs. Trivet led him reluctantly away to answer questions.

Beatrice Canning dozed in a corner by herself. Soon she was going to undress. Undressing in such a situation awakened in her hope and adventurousness. Would Mr. Trivet come in to say good-night to her? Would Professor Seabright? Would both of them come? She was not sure; but there was sufficient doubt about the matter for her to feel much anticipatory and pleasurable excitement. One by one; slowly; languorously, she took off her clothes. The outside layer of clothes was modest, even austere; but the lower she got the more fanciful and frivolous they became, until she reached next to her skin garments as frail and delicate as gossamer which contained her monstrous body precariously, like the skin of a plump sausage.

Her pyjamas were pink with lace trimming round the legs and the neck.

Mr. Trivet leant towards her as he pleaded, "Tell me how sex is arranged here, Miss Canning. I do so want to understand your arrangements. You can't imagine what I've been through with Bella because we haven't known how to arrange things."

His wrinkled elfin face was serious and anxious. Every now and again he moistened his lips with his tongue.

"The quarrels and misunderstandings we've had! The strain of it all! Never knowing how to arrange things. Torn this way and that. It's shaken me to pieces, Miss Canning. Worn me out. Exhausted me. She's had nine children." He mentioned the fact in a whisper as though it was too awful to speak aloud. He seemed to be mutely, agonisedly pointing to himself as the victim of a process. "Look at her," he seemed to be saying; "and then look at me. They haven't left a wrinkle on her. Not a mark. And I'm a reed shaken hither and thither by gusts of emotion; bleached and whitened by consuming lusts; a scarred, disabled victim of a battle that has only invigorated her."

"Yes," he went on, "nine; and she says she'll have more. A thing like that couldn't happen here, could it, Miss Canning?"

Beatrice settled herself in her pillows and cleared her throat. Mr. Trivet's visit was not proceeding precisely along the lines she had envisaged; but still, she was quite ready to be informative about a subject to which she'd given a good deal of thought and study.

"By Soviet law," she began, "a marriage contract can be annulled at the request of either party to it. The State accepts responsibility for all children born; but the father, when he can be identified, is expected to contribute towards the upkeep of his child or children according to his means."

She paused.

"Is that free love?" Mr. Trivet asked incredulously.

Beatrice smiled and said, "It's the framework or machinery. The reality . . ."

"The reality!" Mr. Trivet repeated, trembling with excitement. "Oh! Miss Canning, show me the reality. Show me free love."

He buried his face in her enormous breasts; and her arms engulfed him.

"The reality! They wouldn't let me investigate marriage and birth control. Mrs. T. wanted it. They said I'd have to take on local government. But I'm not interested in local government. I'm interested in sex," he sobbed, his little shoulders heaving and shaking; his face submerged in the mystery of Beatrice's bosom.

There was a knock at the door; and Mr. Trivet only just had time to disinter himself before Professor Seabright came into the compartment.

"We were talking, Professor," Beatrice said, quite unruffled, "about the Soviet marriage system and its ethical basis."

"Very interesting," the Professor answered.

He was a large, white, soft man, the lower part of whose face seemed to be disintegrating as though it had been attacked by some venomous parasite. This was not, however, the case. The face had been so from birth. It was its natural shape.

"I am not," the Professor went on, "a prejudiced person. I like to consider every question on its merits quite apart from traditional prejudices and predispositions. For this reason, and no other, I am regarded in the United States as a dangerous revolutionary. Now in regard to Soviet marriage laws and the Soviet Government's attempts to abolish the family, I have always taken the line . . ."

He continued like this for a considerable time. Beatrice occasionally interpolated an exclamation of agreement; and Mr. Trivet contented himself with just nodding. After an hour the Professor seemed only to be getting into his stride. Mr. Trivet looked anxiously at his watch, and thought anxiously of Mrs. Trivet waiting for him. Could it be, he wondered, that the Professor was waiting for him to go as he was waiting for the Professor to go? If so, he would be disappointed. Nothing should dislodge him. Neither present boredom nor future punishment.

When another hour had passed, Mr. Trivet grew desperate. "I take into account," the Professor was saying, "that the love of the mother for her child; of brother for brother; even of cousin for cousin, have a value. Not only a personal value as ennobling the individual; but a social value as knitting together the members of a society. At the same time, I cannot, dare not, shut my eyes to the fact that . . ."

"I think," Mr. Trivet interrupted emphatically, "that Miss Canning is tired and wants to go to sleep."

His accumulated disappointment and irritation gave his words force. He stood over Professor Seabright; stemmed the flow of his speech, and marshalled him out of the compartment.

Mrs. Trivet was still awake, and made searching enquiries about his movements.

"Fancy," he said reproachfully, "being jealous here of all places! After all our discussions! After all we've said!"

* * * * *

At Kharkov the next morning a band played them into the railway station; and a special guard of honour greeted Kalinin, who was travelling on the train. The little man, bearded, played the part of a public personage with perky dignity. Roden, watching him curiously, thought that he was disappointingly like an alderman opening a new municipal waterworks; and it was only the band's spirited rendering of the "Internationale" that reminded him that he was in the one country where personal pomposity, along with rank and every kind of social and economic inequality, had been abolished.

The journalists and distinguished visitors followed Ouspenski, who led them first to breakfast and then to inspect a factory. They drifted, a rather gloomy procession, from one department to another, staring uncomprehendingly at furnaces and machines, and listening patiently while a polyglot guide explained and extolled.

"And the nursing mothers?" Mrs. Trivet whispered

to Mr. Aarons. They filed into a room where a woman was suckling a baby, and stared at her as they had stared at furnaces and machines.

"Only one?" Mrs. Trivet complained.

Mr. Aarons, at her elbow, pointed out that the women came to feed their babies at different times; just when they felt like it, and that this happened to be an off time. "If we'd come a little earlier, the matron tells me, we'd have seen twenty or more. They like to come in batches because it gives them a chance to gossip," he said archly.

Karl Keightan took notes.

"This is the kind of thing the American public ought to know about," he said to Stoope.

Stoope agreed.

"And remember, gentlemen," Ouspenski orated when they were about to leave, "three years ago there was nothing here at all. It was an open space."

He looked behind him complacently at tall chimneys outlined against the sky. That was what he liked—the general effect; the poster; U.S.S.R. in construction; photographed industry, glossy, picturesque, impressive.

* * * * *

Instead of attending a tea given by the local branch of Vox, Stoope interviewed Stalin's mother. The idea had come to him in the middle of the night. He knew that the mothers, and even grandmothers, of American presidents and film stars had provided enterprising journalists with excellent copy. If presidents and film stars, why not Stalin? he asked himself. Stalin must have a mother somewhere. It was only a question of finding her. He found her; and he interviewed her.

The form of the interview was already in his mind before it took place. There were plenty of precedents. Naturally Mrs. Stalin would be old. Naturally she would have silver grey hair, and spectacles that had a way of falling down her nose. Naturally she would be proud of her famous son, and treasure little mementoes and trophies—a lock of his hair; copies of newspapers containing his photograph and reports of his speeches; a miniature done when he was a dashing young revolutionary and before he had made good. It was important, at the same time, that she should have a mind of her own even though her son did live in the Kremlin and she in a little cottage in the country with a thatched roof and a neat garden that she looked after herself. The old lady, if she was to fill her rôle properly, must have a touch of asperity in her nature, and not wholly approve of the Dictatorship of the Proletariat and its doings.

"If there's any more of this victimisation of kulaks I'll really have to give Jo-Jo a talking to," she ought to say, showing where the son got his determination from. "Why! if it comes to that, I'm a bit of a kulak myself."

While Cooley sat moodily drinking Vox's tea Stoope wrote up his interview:

> Mrs. Stalin was washing up in the kitchen when I arrived. Hearing there was a visitor she took off her apron and received me in the front parlour; a neat homely little room, and all in apple-pie order. She was short with silver-grey hair, and

wore spectacles that had a way of falling down her nose. Her dress was black and prim, and she sat bolt upright in her chair with her hands (I noticed they were roughened with hard work in the house and in the garden) folded in her lap.

"Mrs. Stalin," I said, "I believe this is the first time you've honoured a foreign journalist by giving him an interview."

She nodded and waited for me to go on. She was completely self-possessed; and I felt a little doubtful about how to begin.

"Would you be so good, Ma'am," I said, "as to tell me something about your distinguished son's childhood?"

"Jo-Jo," she answered, "was a good boy. I will never allow a word said against him in this house except, of course, by me. At school he was always top of his class; and the reports I had of him from the Jesuit Seminary where he was undergoing training for the Ministry were invariably excellent."

I noticed a look of sadness in the old lady's face as she referred to her son's interrupted theological studies. There may even have been tears in her eyes. In any case her spectacles grew a little misty; and she took them off and dried them vigorously.

"I don't wish to touch, Ma'am," I said, "on a painful subject; but would it be impertinent on my part to ask why your son left the Jesuit Seminary before graduating?"

"He was delicate and nervous," she answered shortly; and I felt it would be unwise to pursue that topic any further.

After a short silence I asked her whether there were any episodes in his boyhood which gave promise of his future greatness.

She thought for a little while; smiled, and with a mischievous twinkle in her eye replied, "I remember a game he was very fond of. He used to collect the other boys in the village together and tell them they must elect a leader. Then they'd elect him; and he'd make them play only the games he liked, and in the way he liked. He was a very strong character even when he was quite young, my Jo-Jo."

"Having met his mother I can well believe that," I said.

She looked pleased.

"You must," I went on, "be very proud of him."

"Well," she said, "I won't say but what I am. They send me the papers sometimes with his photo and speeches in; and though, mind you, I don't hold with everything he's done, and tell him so when I see him, he was always what we peasants call a trier; and I know he's a trier still."

"I believe, Ma'am," I answered, "that you wouldn't find many to disagree with you there."

"And now," she said, "I must get back to the kitchen or the washing-up'll never be finished, and the dinner'll be spoiled."

She was standing in the doorway when I walked away; a little grey-haired lady dressed in black; the mother of the world's most powerful and most mysterious despot; of peasant stock; somehow reminding me of those Quaker ancestors, those little ladies in grey, from whom President Hoover and so many of our great Americans can trace their descent.

* * * * *

The special train arrived at Dnieprostroi late at night; and Ouspenski suggested that they should go and see the dam and the illuminations at once. Written over the dam in letters of fire was a slogan: "Electricity plus Power equals Communism." Sirens shrieked, and searchlights flashed across the sky. There was a great swirl and rush of water in the river below. Soldiers on sentry-go, their bayonets gleaming, marched backwards and forwards.

Ouspenski climbed on to a little knoll and took off his hat. In the exhilaration of the moment he forgot Lily Jones, and the permanent wave in his hair, and the scent he sprayed over himself every morning and evening. He forgot his delight at sitting in the back seat of a large saloon car, and his pride in his plus-fours, and the magazine covers that decorated the walls of his bedroom. The little group of foreigners round him; parasites; sentimentalists; frustrated revolutionaries; newsmen; neurotics, whom he had been treating with such obsequious consideration, seemed remote and contemptible. They did not understand. They were out of it. He understood. For a moment he became identified with the force that he served and feared. For a moment he was the Dictatorship of the Proletariat. The noise; the flashing lights; the movement; the sense of something immense that was reigned in, controlled; power concentrated into switches that his fingers could turn; enormous wheels and turbines silently, precisely, revolving, or being still as he commanded, intoxicated him. "We have destroyed and now we build," he exulted. "Who dares now to talk of failure or of an experiment in face of this?"

"It surely is very impressive; very impressive indeed," Karl Keightan murmured, ponderously shaking his head; his face suddenly solemn as though, in the middle of a Sunday-school treat, a clergyman had unexpectedly started to pray aloud.

"It surely is," Stoope agreed.

* * * * *

Bolshevism, as Ouspenski boasted, had to destroy. It set out to destroy everything formerly in existence. This meant destroying people because people are indissolubly connected with things. It would mean, if it was carried through to the end, destroying everyone, since people's lives have their roots in the past, and in institutions and customs and beliefs that have grown out of the past. People's lives are part of the past; and if the past is to be destroyed they have to be destroyed as well. The past and people stand or fall together.

Even in Russia, however, the destructive force innate in Bolshevism cannot be carried through to the end. It gains impetus; proceeds more and more frantically and hysterically, but must at last spend itself. It cannot be carried through to the end because it depends on hate. It presupposes a society in a perpetual ferment of hate, or of class war. Certain individuals; sadists and some Jews and cripples; frustrated intellectuals, can hate all their lives; base their lives on hate; and a whole society can be propagandised into hating for the duration, say, of a war or a general election; but no whole society can hate indefinitely. There comes a limit. No whole society can hate long enough to destroy itself; and self-destruction is the only conceivable end of Bolshevism and of the class war. Thus Bolshevism must, by the nature of things and by its own nature, be an uncompleted process.

The process has been carried to unusual lengths in Russia because, by the time the mob was sick of hating, and in a mood to shout, "A bas la guillotine!" the Dictatorship of the Proletariat had created a machinery of destruction which worked independently of the mob, and which, having driven away interventionist armies, could be used, and was used, against the mob. The class war, in fact, became an institution or vested interest. For fear that the class war should die down an organisation was created whose business was to keep it alive by, on the one hand, making class enemies, and, on the other, destroying them. This machinery of destruction is a non-stop puppet revolution. It has its properties and its formulæ and its personnel; its stage army and villain and hero, and serves to perpetuate artificially the circumstances in which alone the Dictatorship of the Proletariat can continue to exist; as though the Church, in order to keep alive the first inspiration out of which its doctrine and its power came, had Jesus nailed on to the cross again and again, the corpse becoming more and more bloodless, putrefied; made a skull contort with agony, and a regimented crowd jeer and deserve punishment while the elect, the apostles, the Dictatorship of the Proletariat, were radiant with electric virtue.

The machinery of destruction works still, clearing away the past; that is, everyone and everything, and making a classless socialist desert in which to realise

Ouspenski's dreams. It is Bolshevism; translated by Mr. Aarons into terms of crèches and abortions for all to edify Mrs. Trivet, and into terms of a seven-hour day and the emancipation of women to edify Mrs. Eardley-Wheatsheaf; translated by Beatrice into terms of free love to edify Professor Seabright and Mr. Trivet; translated by the Comintern into terms of international proletarian solidarity to edify Roden and the I.L.P.; translated by Cooley into terms of headlines to edify the American newspaper reading public; translated by the Commissar for Foreign Affairs into terms of peace and disarmament to edify the League of Nations Union, and into terms of the rhomba to edify himself; seen by Bill very much as it is—his revenge and his exaltation; fire consuming a civilisation he hates, and a chalice out of which he can drink the blood of his enemies.

* * * * *

Standing on a knoll; his hat off and surrounded by foreign journalists and distinguished visitors, it was the realisation of a general idea and not destruction, the process of clearing a space to make room for the general idea, which uplifted Ouspenski's heart. His general idea had grown by accretion; layer upon layer of frustration folding round an inner core of hate and envy; frustration of his appetites because he was poor; frustration of his vanity because he was unintelligent and lazy and ugly and cowardly; frustration of his egotism because he was a Jew. Power swelled the general idea. It became swollen and inflated. Arrogance was added unto it. Instead of existing secretly in his heart, soldiers and armoured cars and tanks, rattling across the Red Square, bore it on their standards and shouted it in their slogans. They would carry it to the uttermost corners of the earth. The general idea, and Ouspenski with it, was fortified and made splendid by power.

Layers of frustration unfolded to form a flower. Ouspenski knew what he wanted. He had lived in Berlin, and worn a suit with a double-breasted waistcoat, and a bowler hat, and a waisted overcoat with padded shoulders. He had seen girls dance in night clubs; and lifts had carried him from one department to another in multiple shops. He had eaten to the music of orchestras, and had been exhilarated by the tumult of electric signs and traffic. Power plus electricity equalled Communism. Ouspenski had inherited the earth, and he knew exactly what the earth must be like for his inheritance to satisfy him; knew the delights that were available for those who sat in the seats of the mighty. Ouspenski plus power equalled a promised land.

What a promised land it was! Horror piled on horror. Abomination of desolation. Jerry-built immensity made and inhabited by slaves. Everything most bestial and most vulgar—barbarian arrogance and salesman servility; humanitarian sentimentality and hypocrisy; rotarian Big Business and Prosperity; *nackt kultur* and pretentious lechery—collected into a heap; an enormous pyramid of filth, in honour of Ouspenski and the Dictatorship of the Proletariat.

The great illuminated dam, and the searchlights in

the sky, and the shriek of the sirens excited Ouspenski. The promised land had come to pass. It was here. His enemies had been scattered; and the whole human race was bowing down in awed admiration before his realised general idea. He saw a paradise of motor-cars, and ready-reckoners, and telephones, and tape machines, and loud-speakers; saw flood-lit smooth roadways, and grey skyscrapers; many mansions, and himself on the right hand of Stalin the father; sitting with the Dictatorship of the Proletariat and watching angels as they built Socialism, and shouted slogans, and processed methodically to and fro.

"You see, gentlemen, what we have done," he shouted. "The largest hydro-electric station in the world. The world's record for cement-pouring. More electricity being generated here than has ever before been generated in one single place. The whole thing finished in under four years. Working now. It is a great moment for us, gentlemen." Karl Keightan took off his hat. It seemed to him to be the right thing to do; and he hoped that the others would follow his example.

"Mr. Ouspenski," he began; "we, representatives of many nations and many newspapers, would like you to know . . ."

*   *   *   *   *

The next morning Kalinin stood with the other notables on a raised platform and addressed a large audience arranged in an amphitheatre. The audience consisted of delegations with their banners and bands.

Every now and again one or other of these bands would play the "Internationale" and the whole audience stand. Photographers hovered round Kalinin's perch like insects with protruding eyes. He delivered a long speech which was echoed by a series of loud-speakers. By his side stood Colonel Ashburton, an American; short and ruddy, and with five quivering chins.

It was a great still ant heap. Kalinin's words, dried by the loud-speakers, rolled over the ant heap like a dry wind. There was no response to his words. Only an occasional rumble of drilled applause; an occasional outburst of the "Internationale." The affair needed darkness broken by searchlights and letters of fire to give it substance. It was ghostly by daylight. Ouspenski's promised land preached by loud-speakers to an orderly ant heap seemed trivial and empty. Even the Commissar for Heavy Industry, an enormous Georgian, failed to enthuse the chilly gathering. Kalinin; peasant president as Cooley always called him; fond of a bottle of champagne and a nice girl from the ballet; scrubby disorderly look of an under-secretary of state for something or other, droned on and on like a village priest mumbling a familiar prayer.

Better the dam as statistics in the Opera House or on a hoarding than the dam itself on a cold November morning. Better rouged and powdered Soviet athletes building an imaginary dam with imaginary hammers to the tune of "If you were the only girl in the world" than row upon row of the ants that had built the dam. Ouspenski felt suddenly tired. After all, it had been a long journey, and his flock was tiresome. Soon it'll all be over, he thought thankfully; and I'll be back in Moscow, and see Lily again. The magic of the evening before had quite departed; and the stone wall across the River Dnieper was grim and uninteresting.

There was for Cooley only one possible lead:

"BOLSHEVIK PEASANT PRESIDENT HONOURS AMERICAN ENGINEER."

In his telegram he described how at a certain point in the proceedings Kalinin pinned the Order of the Red Banner on to Colonel Ashburton's breast; how as he did so the bands struck up all together, and how he, Cooley, saw in the episode a promise of closer cultural and economic relations between two great progressive peoples.

*   *   *   *   *

Stoope slipped off to have a drink with Camshott, another American engineer; a giant, ruddy, with small blue eyes; blond hair growing thickly on the back of his hands and in tufts on his fingers, and long silky hairs drooping down from his cheek bones.

"It's a swell dam," Stoope said.

"It sure is," Camshott answered.

"How do you like working in Russia?" Stoope asked, eager to gather yet another viewpoint.

"Fine," the other answered. "You can do what you like here. Build what you like, and as big as you like. The bigger the better. No restrictions on anything. Only get on with the job. Get it finished no matter what it costs; no matter how many hours you or anyone else has to work. Yes, I like it. It's a big country; and these boys have got big ideas. I'm proud to work for them. Yes, sir, proud to be in on this show."

Stoope felt timid in his company. He was like a little man with a big dog. "Good boy! Good boy!"

"The food shortage?" he ventured to ask.

"I don't know much about that," Camshott answered. "I live on cans. Bad for the teeth."

He opened his mouth to show brown, decayed fangs.

Stoope had thought of him somehow as living on raw flesh. It surprised him that such an enormous frame and such vitality could be kept going on cans.

"The workers?" he asked timidly. "Do they get enough to eat?"

"I guess they do. I guess they must. Otherwise they couldn't work so hard."

"Do you get any forced labour? Politicals and so on."

Camshott nodded. He was not going to be forced into being apologetic. Stoope, avoiding his eye, remembered with relief Jefferson's viewpoint.

"After all," he said, "you can't make omelettes without breaking eggs."

"You sure can't," the other agreed.

They had another drink and opened a can.

*   *   *   *   *

A wave of salesmanship massed itself to wash over Russia. On the top of the wave sat Lord Edderton.

"I want you to tell us exactly what you'd like to see," Mr. Aarons said to him when he first arrived in

Moscow. "People often complain that we only show visitors what we want them to see. You can go anywhere you like and see anything you like. Our failures and mistakes (they are many and lamentable) are as open to inspection as our successes."

It might have been Mr. Aarons in striped trousers and black cut-away coat standing by the main entrance of a multiple store. "What can we show you, sir? Our motto is service. Infant welfare, sir? Certainly; second floor and first on the right. Perhaps you'd care to see our special display of socialist construction in the roof garden? No one's going to try and persuade you to buy anything. Just see for yourself."

Lord Edderton said that he was specially interested in heavy industry; and Mr. Aarons made a note of the fact on a piece of paper.

He began with the nine turbines at Dnieprostroi. They were revolving in a tall power station. An American engineer sometimes listened to one or other of them like a doctor listening to a heart.

"What are they driving?" Lord Edderton asked in an awed whisper.

His interpreter answered that for the moment they weren't driving anything. On tour his manner suggested more a restaurant car attendant than a waiter. He served up heavy industry gymnastically; with less ceremony than he served up propaganda in Moscow, but with more zest. There was something breathless, dynamic, about the way he fed Lord Edderton on the actual stuff of the Five-Year Plan.

"It's good," he said, "for them to turn like that for a

year or so. By the time we're ready with plant for them to drive they'll be nicely run in."

Lord Edderton, thinking of a new car he had lately bought, agreed that it would be as well to run them in before putting any great strain on them.

The power station was grey and cool like a cathedral. It was a mansion in Ouspenski's promised land; and the turbines, generating power for the Dictatorship of the Proletariat, were an angelic choir intoning hymns of praise; the orchestra playing in the basement of Mr. Aarons's multiple store and soothing buyers into making purchases; soothing Lord Edderton.

As the wave of showmanship washed him from one heavy industry to another he made up speeches to be delivered later in the House of Lords. His sleepy brother peers should know about this new world where factories and power stations and blast furnaces sprang up like mushrooms in the night. He would tell them.

Between one heavy industry and another there was nothing; a waste of space; ether through which, it seemed to Lord Edderton, he travelled with the speed of thought, closing his eyes in Dnieprostroi and opening them in Magnetogorsk, and beginning, breathless, to inspect another giant of socialist construction. The giants themselves were the merest beginning. Plans and figures, whose magnitude intoxicated him, filled in like dreams the long journeys across Russia. Future prospects were illimitable. The multiple store, growing upward into the sky, added to itself storey after storey, department after department, until its roof merged into heaven.

Lord Edderton felt himself translated into a fairyland. Tiresome and, to him, incomprehensible details that made business and politics such a drudgery at home no longer mattered. The multiple store kept no register of petty cash. It was built on bigger, more majestic lines than any Woolworth's or Selfridge's. He did not need to understand anything. Only to feel. To give himself to the ebb and flow of the wave of showmanship on which he rode. His brother peers, he knew, did not appreciate his talents. They had persistently refused to take him seriously. In their company he felt diffident and uneasy. Here it was different. He threw out his chest and tightened up his mouth. Let them take care. Let them remember what had happened to their like in Russia. When the structure was finished and on view for all the world to see they would be swept away, and he who had understood and prophesied the wrath to come would be numbered amongst the elect.

Once a doubt came to him. "I want to see more people and less machinery," he said to his interpreter. "I want to see how they live and work and play so that I can tell working-class audiences in England about the things that interest them."

"You shall," the interpreter promised him.

They were sitting together in Lord Edderton's special first-class coach.

("No mutton chops today, sir; but what about an omelette? Won't you let me make you an omelette?")

"Meanwhile," the interpreter went on, "let me give you a few figures."

By the time he had finished giving a few figures Lord Edderton had a lot of interesting material to put before working-class audiences. He knew, for instance, how the Dictatorship of the Proletariat had steadily increased wages. He knew the amount of bread and milk and butter and meat and eggs consumed per head of population. He knew the available living space in cubic metres in the most important Russian cities. He knew in the most precise detail the provision the Dictatorship of the Proletariat had made for recreation and study, for the general cultural well-being of the toiling masses. It was thus scarcely necessary for him to see all this for himself. Being, however, a conscientious person, he insisted on visiting a factory worker's home, and on eating a meal in a factory restaurant, and on spending an evening in an Institute for Culture and Rest to corroborate the interpreter's figures.

The wave of showmanship at last deposited him, tired but radiant, in Moscow. "When I get back to England," he said to Mr. Aarons, "I'm going to get together a few of the more intelligent of those who've visited Russia and see whether we can't make our influence felt on public opinion. We ought to be able to do something towards counteracting the more ridiculous of the scare stories that get into the Press; and, of course, I shall make a point of speaking in the House of Lords about your wonderful experiment."

*   *   *   *   *

Lord Edderton got together a few of the more intelligent visitors to Russia as he had promised Mr. Aarons; and they formed themselves into a society called the We Saw the Soviets Fellowship. At the first meeting Mrs. Trivet read a paper on Maternity Care, Contraception and Abortion in the U.S.S.R., which was greatly appreciated. Mr. Trivet was in an unruly mood. "Would we go and live in Russia?" he asked vehemently. "That's the real test. Would we stand it for a month? Of course we wouldn't." Then he caught Mrs. Trivet's eye and broke off abruptly.

"The gibe about not going to Russia is an old one," the editor of the *Weekly Socialist* retorted. "For my part I feel that we're much more use here trying to enlighten the masses about the real state of affairs in Russia, and undoing as far as we can the pernicious effects of the lies and distortions spread by a corrupt capitalist Press." He was dark and sallow. Hair fell like darkness over his face. Each week he raked over what had happened in the world, arranging it in patterns, defining the attitude towards it of the righteous and the pure of heart. "In my own particular case I can without boasting claim that the *Weekly Socialist* is little by little preparing the British public for the great social upheaval that we know to be inevitable."

Did it mean, the others wondered, that he was prepared to receive articles from them? Was that his service to the cause of revolution? If so they could conceive no better.

Mrs. Eardley-Wheatsheaf, who had other means of marketing articles, sniffed contemptuously.

"Your paper," she said, "is written by the converted and read by the converted. My book..."

Her book! They looked at one another. She was ready with her book. She had stolen a march on them. She was going to be first in the field.

"My book will be ready in the spring. I shall pay a flying visit to Moscow to show it to that very clever young man Mr. Aarons to make sure I haven't made any mistakes. I shall publish it at three shillings and sixpence. It will reach the masses."

"We are trying the experiment of circulating a certain number of copies of the *Weekly Socialist* gratis in the East End," the editor said weakly. He was afraid of Mrs. Eardley-Wheatsheaf.

* * * * *

Lord Edderton waited patiently for his chance in the House of Lords. He had his speech ready; and he sat, expectant, through uninteresting debates waiting to deliver it. How he would make his brother peers sit up! How he would shock them, and shake them out of their complacency. How absurd they seemed sitting there unaware of the marvellous things taking place at their very doorstep!

A debate on foreign affairs gave him his opportunity. As he warmed to his subject a slight lisp in his speech became more pronounced. His pale blue eyes flashed; and his arms made extravagant gestures. "At Dnieprostroi the largest hydro-electric station in the world. Great industrial cities springing up in the wastes of Siberia. Enormous collective farms with regiments of tractors marshalled for work like an army on manœuvres."

His brother peers continued to loll in their places, and the Lord Chancellor to drowse on his woolsack. Their indifference infuriated Lord Edderton. Why weren't they interested? Why didn't what he had seen stir them as it had stirred him? He poured out the vision that had come to him in the vacuum between one giant of socialist construction and another; in the vacuum between Lenin's pink head and the staring proletariat; in the vacuum between Ouspenski's general idea and life bubbling up into people and trees and crops and cities and civilisations. The vacuum was a white cinema screen on to which his vision was projected. A two-dimensional vision. A thing of light and shadows. A nothingness. "You may be indifferent now," he shouted, a lisping prophet; "but when the pwesent cowupt social order falls about your ears, and the iwesistible forces of wevolution surge up to engulf you, then you will wealise the magnitude and significance of what has been achieved in Wussia."

The response to his speech was disappointing. Near him sat a trade union leader who had been given a peerage by the last Labour Government. The man had an enormous red face; and he was laughing at Lord Edderton's speech. His huge stomach and the folds of his chin were shaking as he listened to it.

* * * * *

Dr. and Mrs. Golden lived in the Metropole Hotel. Dr. Golden was a chemist, and employed by the

Dictatorship of the Proletariat in connection with the manufacture of poison gas. They had a pink and gold suite of rooms: very ornate, and full of mirrors. Mrs. Golden had rearranged the furniture and brought in one or two things of her own to make the place, as she said, more homely. She had red hair and a red and white face. Dr. Golden was massive and sallow. His face was rather like poison gas; cloudy; features undefined; but the whole effect strong and in its acrid venomous way intelligent. They had brought a Rolls-Royce car with them into Russia; and in this they rode about the streets of Moscow. They were very fond of tomatoes; and each evening after dinner they ate a tin of them out of tumblers with a spoon.

Mrs. Golden, who had a tender heart, often spoke to Dr. Golden while they were eating their tomatoes about the unhappy hungry look of the people she saw when she looked out of the window of their Rolls-Royce car.

"You have to remember, my dear," he would say, patting her shoulder, "that it's like a war. In a war there are casualties, aren't there? You can't avoid casualties in a war, can you?"

She would nod her agreement.

"Well," he would continue triumphantly, "there's a war going on here; and we people who are in the front line trenches working on socialist construction (his voice was even and undramatic but forceful) are determined to win whatever the cost may be. As Mr. Jefferson said the other night, you can't make omelettes without cracking eggs. That's all there is to it."

"I suppose it is," Mrs. Golden would agree. "But

even so I don't quite understand which is eggs and which is omelette, and who's cracking what."

"Of course you don't, bless you," Dr. Golden would say, giving her a kiss and finishing the last spoonful of tomato.

CHAPTER IV
ASH-BLOND INCORRUPTIBLE

"Lenin a compris que les révolutions n'étaient point une question de doctrine, mais un drame de la faim, et que la conquête du pain en réglait le cours, en dictait la tactique, en imposait les dogmes, suivant l'époque et les circonstances." — HENRY ROLLIN

"Lenin understood that revolutions were not a question of doctrine but a tragedy of hunger, and that the acquisition of bread in regulating the course, in dictating tactics, in imposing dogmas, follows the times and the circumstances." — HENRY ROLLIN

CHAPTER IV
ASH-BLOND INCORRUPTIBLE

"THERE'S a lot of talk," the editor of a great English newspaper said to Wilfred Pye, " going about of a famine in Russia. You might just go and see if there's anything in it."

Damp strips of proof were spread over the desk between them: "The Situation in Spain"; "The Situation in China."

Pye, booted and spurred, loins girt for a journey, touched a forelock and said, " Ay, ay, sir."

He stumped away in corduroy breeches to see if there was anything in it. His luggage could be fastened on to his back; all his possessions folded up intricately. Even when he sat at dinner in the restaurant car of a European express he seemed to be foraging; hands reaching out over a camp-fire; old burnt pipe slowly filled; eyes meditative. He bivouacked in Pullman coaches, and lived a nomad in the midst of civilisation.

He was venerable and blond. Long hair was draped round a lofty pate. The pate, a pink remote peak, towered above his face; and his mouth was hidden by a silky walrus moustache whose strands trembled and agitated when he laughed. How many subject peoples struggling to be free had reason to venerate him! To them his glowing pate had been a lamp of hope shining through the darkness of their oppression. How many exploiters of backward races had reason to hate and fear him! To them his glowing pate had been a danger signal, a warning that their evil enterprises would not be tolerated for ever.

The Soviet Ambassador in London gave him lunch at Simpson's before he started off to see if there was anything in it.

"We have suffered a great deal," the Ambassador said, "at the hands of foreign journalists; and it is a great relief to us that a journalist like yourself, with an international reputation for integrity, and representing a newspaper with an international reputation for integrity, should be paying a visit to our Union."

Pye chuckled, and the strands of his moustache, heavy with soup, waved languidly.

"You can be sure," he answered, "that I'll see things for myself and write about them as they are."

"That's all we want," the Ambassador said.

He had a little tight mouth. Despite its smallness (just a tiny spot on a grey expanse of face) he seemed always to be hiding behind it as though, like a camera aperture, it focussed his entire personality.

Neither Pye nor the Ambassador was talkative; and it was not until he had nearly finished a helping of duck that Pye said, "My editor wants me particularly to investigate the food situation. There have been a lot of stories going about."

"I need scarcely say false stories," the Ambassador said.

"Of course, false," Pye said.

There was another pause, extending till the savoury.

"False doesn't mean, I take it, that you haven't had your difficulties?" Pye said.

"Difficulties are one thing and famine is another," the Ambassador said, ordering two brandies.

"Of course," Pye said, sipping his brandy.

*   *   *   *   *

Pye had a simple mind. Its simplicity was its strength, because it meant that any one idea existing alone in it found forcible expression. The one idea existing alone in it now was food. Obviously, Pye thought, I must see where people eat; how they eat, and what they eat. I must go to restaurants and note their prices, and visit markets, and board for a few days with a private family, and collect statistics about rations. There were certain facts, the truth; and it was his business to present these facts, this truth, to the readers of a great English Liberal newspaper, and through it to humane enlightened opinion generally. He had no doubts about his integrity in the matter. I go to Russia, he thought, with an open mind. He saw himself as a reed through which truth whistled in weighty emphatic sentences.

Although his mind was simple it had a background. This background had grown up slowly; and now he was incapable of seeing the world except against it. The world apart from this background had no existence. His thoughts pierced it like light rays a lens, and were bent and coloured; and the amount of their deflection and the colour they took on did not vary, being dependent on the construction of the background which was a constant. Thus he moved towards minorities as sufferers from agoraphobia move towards a wall. Thus he preferred the weak to the strong, and aspiration to achievement, and persecution to popularity. His rôle was to be a voice crying in the wilderness; and where no wilderness existed for him to cry in he made one.

Bolshevism seen against his mind's background was a cause, and therefore admirable. It was unconquerable soul. It was the ideal valiantly existing in a hostile world. It was the future; hated by all save the far-seeing and the pure of heart; hated by all save Pye and his great English Liberal newspaper. Like Bill, he favoured the exaltation of the humble and meek; but not because he was humble and meek himself and wanted to be exalted; because it was a mental habit with him to associate righteousness with weakness. It was inconceivable that he should have considered the matter otherwise. To have done so would have been to play against his own side. He had served his side faithfully for many years; had grown old and full of honour in its service, and would go on serving it until he died. An old salt; venerable with championing good causes; a veteran with a long and honourable record of fighting for the weak and the oppressed, when he looked at a map it was not countries he saw, but wrongs sprawling across five continents.

*　　*　　*　　*　　*

The restaurant in his Moscow hotel seemed well stocked. No lack of food here, he thought, and began to write an introductory article:

"Superficially at least there are no signs of famine. People in the streets are well nourished. I have just finished an excellent meal which cost me the equivalent of two shillings. It does not do, however, to jump to conclusions. . . ."

A paragraph in special type appeared at the head of the article when it was published to the effect that, in view of reports that had been current about a food shortage in Russia, a special correspondent, Wilfred Pye, was investigating the situation. At last, the readers of the great English Liberal newspaper thought, breathing a sigh of relief, we shall get the facts impartially presented. They were accustomed to look to their newspaper and to Wilfred Pye to clear up doubtful issues of the kind.

Ouspenski looked at Pye across a wide desk. He smiled ingratiatingly as he said, " We are proud, Mr. Pye, to have you amongst us. Your name, and the name of the newspaper you represent, are, I can assure you, more a recommendation here than perhaps anywhere else in the world, which is saying a lot. If there is any way in which I can be of use to you I hope you will let me know."

Pye accepted this homage as his due. His blond moustache was smooth and untroubled like the fur of a contented cat. Governments often enough had been hostile and suspicious; but it was fitting that the Dictatorship of the Proletariat should take him at once to its bosom.

" I want to meet a few people," he said.

Ouspenski was all attention. He leant over the desk

as though it was a counter; rubbed his hands together, and seemed to be saying, "Anyone you like, sir; commissar, soldier, sailor, peasant, worker, foreign diplomat or journalist, all at your disposal."

"Not, you understand, official people," Pye went on. "I want to keep away from embassies and journalists."

Ouspenski smiled understandingly. "Of course, a man of taste like yourself wouldn't want me to show him anything but a genuine article," he seemed to be saying.

"First of all," Pye said, "I'd like to meet an Englishman with advanced views who's been living here for some years in an unofficial capacity. Do you know of such a person?" Ouspenski beamed. "By a lucky chance," he seemed to be saying, "I've got the very thing you want in stock."

"I think you'd better meet Mr. Muskett," he said. There was, as he spoke the name, a tinge of patronage, even of contempt, in his voice. Our Mr. Muskett.

Pye went in a tram to Muskett's house. A dense mass of people pushed themselves like toothpaste through the tram's narrow body and out at the end; limbs, bodies, flattened against one another to form a dark streaming fluid; smell of human beings a thick mist in the air. What a lark! Pye thought, and planned to write a droll light article about riding in trams in Moscow. Here, he thought drolly, is the collective man we've heard so much about. The individual merged in the mass. Society, and not the single man or woman, the unit. What a lark! he thought again. And how the readers of the great English Liberal newspaper will chuckle when they read about it!

Muskett lived in a little room by himself. Pye found him sitting on a camp bed. He had taken off his heavy Russian boots, and his socks were stale. There was no shirt underneath his velveteen jacket, so that sometimes, when he leant forwards and the jacket gaped, an expanse of chest showed. His flowing beard and shaven head made him look monkish; a lewd, ribald old monk, lazy and grimy and depraved.

Pye and Muskett looked at one another with understanding. They recognised at once, despite their differences (the one venerable and the other decayed; ash-blond incorruptible and unkempt idealist), a common origin. The very books ranged round the walls made Muskett's dingy room for Pye a home from home. Browning, Ruskin, Emerson, Edward Carpenter, gave to the room's disorder an inward glow of truth and principle; Cole and Maurice Dobb and the Webbs and Hindus brightened the glow with contemporary fire. The two old men, standing up and facing one another, might have been chanting a credo: "We believe in freedom and in progress; we love nature and human intercourse unhindered by outworn conventions; we think that our ideas and aspirations are the basis of, and have found their most perfect expression through, the Dictatorship of the Proletariat as established in the first great Workers' Republic," or intoning a letter to the editor of the *New Statesman* or the *Manchester Guardian*:

"We the undersigned believe it is time that people of good will," etc., etc.

Muskett fetched out a bottle of thick sweet wine; and they sat side by side on his camp bed drinking and talking.

"Now take my case," Muskett said. "I earn . . ."

The word seemed to stiffen both of them. They ceased to loll when it was spoken.

"I earn anything from five to six hundred roubles a month; and I eat in restaurants. Prices have, I admit, risen lately; but I can still get a tolerable meal with meat for ten roubles."

The tone of his voice and Pye's complacent nod suggested that he was recommending a cheap pension.

"The only trouble is," he went on, "that I don't have butter."

He shook his head mournfully. It was a serious thing for him not to have butter.

"I must own," he seemed to be saying, "that I have one, and only one, serious charge against the Dictatorship of the Proletariat; it doesn't provide me with butter."

Pye, sympathetic, admitted the gravity of the charge.

Later in the evening an Indian looked in for a chat. Pye had a special manner for dealing with Orientals. He was benign and fatherly and indulgent, and shook his head as though to say, "There, there; don't take it too much to heart. I quite understand how you feel; and if you'll just leave things to me I'll see you aren't downtrodden any more."

"You'll find," Muskett whispered, "their way of dealing with the colour problem very interesting and illuminating."

"I'm sure I shall," Pye whispered back; "and thank you for the tip. I'll get an article out of it."

The Indian took his place between them on the camp bed. He looked rather tired. His face was grey instead of brown; and his large black eyes were frozen.

"This is Wilfred Pye," Muskett said. "You've heard of him, I suppose?"

"Oh yes," the Indian answered.

Pye seemed to overhang the Indian. His blond hair and moustache seemed to enfold him like a vestment.

"Now," he said gently, "tell me how you find things here."

"Very interesting. Oh! very interesting indeed. I am studying at the Lenin Institute."

He hung his head shyly; and his slim body drooped like a flower.

"I am a revolution," he went on. "The only trouble is (his mouth crumpling with petulant disgust) the food doesn't suit me."

"Do you get enough?" Pye asked.

"Not quite," the Indian answered, looking sideways at Muskett.

Muskett took the situation in hand. He was stern. "Tell us exactly what you get. No generalities. How much bread. How much meat. How much sugar."

The Indian was frightened. Pye's blond hair and Muskett's tangled beard seemed to be closing in on him like a suffocating mist.

"I don't know exactly how much I get," he said weakly. "Only sometimes there doesn't seem to be quite enough."

After he had gone Muskett said, "He's a vegetarian and fussy about his food."

"Quite so," Pye answered.

*   *   *   *   *

The next evening Pye went out in search of markets. In a small street he found a little crowd of people buying and selling. They drifted up and down the street like a wave washing up and down a beach, while two policemen blew whistles and tried to disperse them. Some were clutching things in their hands: fragments of fish and cooked meat; a loaf of bread; a few potatoes. Others were looking for things to buy. The bread was pulpy from much handling; and the fish and meat stank. Deals took place like embraces. The ebb and flow of the crowd threw a buyer into a seller's arms, and when they separated what had been in the seller's hands was in the buyer's. The crowd moved to the rhythm of its exchanges; and its whispered haggling made a melancholy confused hum.

Pye joined in the crowd's movement. He, too, caught its rhythm; knew when to move and when to pause; played to the policemen's whistles as though the buying and selling was a game with rules and a score, and the policemen referees. How very Russian it all is! he thought. What fun! All such fun!

He saw a piece of sausage change hands. The buyer, a bearded peasant, stuffed it greedily into his mouth; then, as he gobbled, retched. Something in his face as he gobbled and retched; something animal, desperate, fearful; appetite and disgust mingled in the two actions of gobbling and retching, brought a sudden doubt into Pye's mind. The man is starving, he thought. Were the others starving? Was there the same look in their eyes as in his? Were they, like him, pale and agonised with starvation? Was this market a kind of scavenging; like cats he had seen in the very early morning in Cairo working ferociously through heaps of garbage? Were they famished animals fighting over refuse?

The doubt haunted him on his way back to his hotel. He saw hunger everywhere; in the faces that hurried past him, and in the patient queues, and in the empty shops, dimly lighted and decorated with red streamers, whose windows contained only busts of Marx and Lenin and Stalin. Stone busts exposed to ravenous eyes. Instead of bread, the law and the prophets offered as tasty morsels to a famished population.

Pye thought things out over dinner. In the first place it was absurd to imagine that the Dictatorship of the Proletariat would serve such an excellent meal to him, a foreigner, if their own people were going short; and he had to balance Muskett against what he had seen. He must keep his head. Not get hysterical. The great English Liberal newspaper wanted facts, the truth, and not impressions or sudden emotional reactions. The market he had seen was obviously illicit. Otherwise why should the police have been trying to disperse it? That is to say, it was patronised by ex-bourgeois and kulak elements. Certainly not by the real workers. As for the shops, one of the charms of Moscow was the lack of salesmanship. In capitalist countries the public fancy had to be tickled by shop-window dressing and advertisement; here, as Ouspenski had explained, distribution was more rationally organised through consumers' co-operatives. In any case, the market he had seen was one amongst many, and therefore not adequate material for generalisations.

In his bedroom, a good dinner and half a bottle of wine inside him, he saw things more coolly than in the streets. He wrote his second article:

> "Unquestionably there is a shortage of certain foods, especially of butter, whose lack is seriously felt. The chief sufferers, however, are members of the old Tzarist aristocracy and bourgeoisie, and those peasants who have obstinately refused to join the collective system. They buy and sell in the streets when they can evade the vigilance of the police. The high prices charged and the poor quality of the food offered for sale in such illegal markets are very noticeable. It must always be remembered, however, that the patrons of these markets are outcastes who, through prejudice or stupidity, have been unable to fit into the new social system. The ordinary Soviet citizen has his co-operative that is well stocked with all the necessaries of life, and whose prices are fixed. He also has his factory restaurant. A visitor only accustomed to the ostentatious display of capitalist marketing might easily imagine that the Moscow shops were all empty, and assume therefore that the population was impoverished. This is not the case. It is perhaps a little difficult for faddy people to get along; and the Government has pursued a policy of not catering for luxury tastes. On the other hand, there is plenty of good simple whole-

some food available for the ordinary worker or peasant; that is, for at least ninety-five per cent. of the population; and I find Soviet circles full of optimism about the prospects for the next harvest. So much for Moscow. Tomorrow I leave for the provinces. I should like in closing to touch on a matter which I shall hope to treat at some length hereafter. I refer to the exemplary manner in which the Soviet Government has handled minority and colour questions. . . ."

* * * * *

Famine is something quite peculiar. It concentrates all effort and thought and feeling on one thing. It makes everyone a frustrated glutton. In a famished town, as in a cheap restaurant, there is always a flavour of food in the air. Everyone brooding on food makes a smell which hangs about them like the smell of gravy and cabbage about a dirty table-cloth. Somehow famine goes beyond hunger, and puts in each face a kind of lewdness; a kind of grey unwholesome longing. People's white gums and mouldering flesh suggest rather a consuming disease like leprosy than appetite. They seem diseased, even evil, rather than pathetic. Their eyes are greedy and restless, and linger greedily, it sometimes seems, on one another's bodies. Their skin gets unnaturally dry and their breath parched and stale like air in a cellar.

In the country famine is more listless. A slowing down of activity. At last a stoppage or blight. Starving peasants are dazed and resigned. They accept famine as a natural calamity, and, up to a point, suffer it patiently. Many die of starvation; but in their eyes such deaths are impersonal like a failure of the crops. They bury their dead in the same spirit and with the same emotions that they clear the fields of spoilt grain, and wait for the next harvest, hoping that they will be able to resist the temptation to gorge themselves on green unripened stalks which, eaten after a famished winter, swell up their bodies and engender a fatal disease.

The famine now raging in Russia is different from any that has hitherto happened because it is organised from within. No external cause like bad weather or a blockade can be blamed for it. People feel it to be a consequence of an inward corruption. It seems to them to be innate in Bolshevism and a fruit of the Dictatorship of the Proletariat. This makes their despair the more hopeless. They see the Dictatorship of the Proletariat going over the country like a flight of locusts, taking away or destroying everything edible and leaving behind a barren wilderness. They hear the Dictatorship of the Proletariat, with fatuous statistical complacency, hail the locust flight as a great achievement, a sublime victory. They feel in themselves the aptness of the famine; its inevitability, and see in the future only an intensification of their present misery.

Marxism, the Dictatorship of the Proletariat's religion, is the most urban religion that has ever existed. It was born in underground printing presses, in dingy lodgings and cafés and hotels. Its prophets were wanderers from one European capital to another whose dreams, like themselves, were rootless. The embodiment of their dreams in Ouspenski's promised land is nothing. As transitory and unreal as American prosperity, or yo-yo, or the Brain Trust. Their real significance is the struggle with earth; with the nature of things and people; with life itself, that their embodiment involves. It alone reveals their real character, their real horror.

This struggle has gone on for fifteen years; sometimes intensifying and sometimes dying down; but steadily, drearily, turning Russia into a battlefield. A people, as it were, self-blockaded. War by the proletariat for the proletariat on the proletariat. A class war. Lenin called it a struggle for bread. In fact, it is rather a struggle against than for bread.

The Dictatorship of the Proletariat sent an army to conquer bread, and it destroyed bread. It went to make the fields yield more abundantly, and it trampled the fields into barrenness. Its banners shut out the sun and prevented crops from ripening. Its slogans rolled over the land like a destroying wind. Its gloomy Marxist thoughts were a heavy mist choking the life out of peasants and animals and soil. It spread death, famine and destruction everywhere.

*   *   *   *   *

Pye travelled third-class because he wanted, as he explained in his articles, to be in contact with real people and not with officials or visitors or privileged persons. Next to him in his compartment was a young man in a peaked uniform hat and an overcoat with brass buttons who knew a little English. He was, he explained to Pye, a member of the Communist party, and on his way to a sanatorium for a rest cure.

"Very nervous," he said, and indicated by twitching his eyes and trembling that he was suffering from neurasthenia.

"Overwork?" Pye suggested.

The young man nodded.

These young people, Pye thought, throw themselves with amazing enthusiasm into the great effort that is being made here to reconstruct human society. It stands to reason that they must sometimes have breakdowns. But what a refreshing type compared with our cynical, pleasure-loving young people in England! He decided that he would write an article about Soviet Youth. He loved writing about Youth, and had written articles in the past on Chinese Youth and Indian Youth and Egyptian Youth. The older he got the more he tended to become the mouthpiece of Youth in all parts of the world.

The young man in the peaked uniform hat told Pye in broken sentences a lot about the Five-Year Plan, and the giants of socialist construction, and the blocks of workers' flats, and the clubs and rest homes. "Big, big business," he said. "Oh! very big."

Pye smiled understandingly. "I quite understand what you mean," he said; then, speaking gently as though he wanted to be tactful in touching on a delicate subject, asked, "What about the food shortage?"

"Food shortage?" the young man echoed, and laughed. Pye laughed with him. They chuckled merrily together.

Three peasants on the opposite seat; one old and the

others not so old; perhaps his sons, watched Pye eat an orange. He peeled it slowly and threw the peel piece by piece into a spittoon. The peasants seemed fascinated by the spectacle of Pye eating an orange, and followed each of his movements with their eyes. He finished the orange and dried his fingers and mouth with a handkerchief.

"Food shortage?" the young man said. "Not at all. Very big business, but no food shortage. Cheliabinsk, Dnieprostroi, Magnetogorsk, Stalingrad, Gorki . . ."

He reeled off the names like a familiar litany.

"No food shortage," he went on, smiling reassuringly.

"Quite so. Quite so," Pye nodded.

The peasants were looking now at the orange peel. The one nearest to the spittoon leant forwards; not deliberately, but casually, as though he was just changing his position. As he leant forwards his hand went nearer and nearer to the spittoon; suddenly made a dart and clutched the orange peel. He ate it up ravenously, giving none to his two companions.

"I think I'll read a bit now," Pye said; irritated; a little uneasy, and took out his Hazlitt.

Letters of introduction took him from place to place. "I don't want you to show me anything," he said everywhere. "Just lend me a motor-car and an interpreter and I'll see for myself." The motor-car would carry him to a collective farm, and the director of the collective farm would tell him how much land had been sown, and how much was to be sown in the spring, and show him collective farm-workers who would tell him, through his interpreter, how happy they were, and how they had everything they wanted. Sometimes it seemed to him that the collective farm-workers did not look quite as contented and happy as they said they were; and, although he knew nothing about farming, he could not help thinking that the fields were in rather poor condition. Even so, like Lord Edderton, the sense of moving from one centre of activity to another kept him excited and appreciative. He too overlooked the intervening spaces, and built in his mind an imaginary Russia with imaginary people and industries and farms. What vision! he thought. What courage! What vitality! and missed the trees for the wood.

* * * * *

Once his motor-car broke down; and since it was a pleasant evening he walked on alone while it was being repaired. He saw a village ahead; white houses with thatched roofs clustering round a domed church on a hill. I'll go into one or two of the houses, he thought, and ask questions. The village was quite silent. There was no life or movement in it. The doors of the houses swung open; chimneys were smokeless and gardens neglected. It was a dead village, and Pye was looking at its corpse. He felt anxious and afraid. How did a dead village come to be there in the middle of a fertile plain? What terrible calamity had driven away all the population? The place, equipped for abundance yet empty of people and produce, was indescribably melancholy. Pye hurried on. He wanted to leave it behind him.

Outside the church he saw a stone monument; painted red and capped with a bust of Stalin. Rain had washed off some of the paint, and a faded paper-chain flapped round it. By the monument stood a man; and Pye attempted to ask him in fragmentary Russian why the village was deserted. The man answered in English. He had a black trimmed beard; and his lips, amongst it, were unnaturally red and his cheeks unnaturally white. His whole appearance was unreal, fantastic; and his hands when he spoke made restless, agitated gestures.

"My parents lived here," he said. "I came to see them. No one is left."

Pye hated and feared the man. His red lips were blood and his pale cheeks were death. As he spoke he seemed to populate the village.

"I was told that the whole village had been exiled; and I couldn't believe it; and I came to see."

Pye expected him to decompose into blood and death in front of the little shoddy monument.

"What do you mean?" Pye asked petulantly.

"Sent away. To the North. To Siberia. Are you a foreign journalist?"

Pye nodded.

"What paper?"

He told him what paper; and the man spat venomously.

"Tell them abroad about this village. Describe it to them." He was losing control of himself. Words came pouring out of him. "How many such villages! No bread anywhere. Everyone dying and swelling up.

Tell them abroad not to buy our food. Tell them Russia is a desert. Tell them how we're suffering."

He was working up to some fearful climax. Pye turned away. He heard thankfully in the distance the sound of a motor-car. When he looked round the man had gone.

Pye asked his interpreter why the village was deserted.

"Collectivisation," the interpreter answered, "has involved a certain redistribution of population."

"Quite so," Pye answered.

Obviously, he thought, the man was a lunatic. A certain type of journalist would have taken him seriously; and (smiling complacently) that's just how scare stories get about.

The same evening Pye went to see a local Soviet official. The electric light was for some reason not working; and the official was sitting behind a branched candlestick. His gold teeth shone in the flickering candle light.

"Sir Pye," he said, "I'm delighted to see you."

Pye bowed. "Not Sir Pye," he murmured. "Just Pye."

"The spring sowing campaign," the official went on, "is going very well."

"I'm delighted to hear it," Pye said.

"The peasants are full of enthusiasm."

Pye nodded.

"We shall sow two-point-three times the acreage sown last year; and the average yield per acre will be increased by forty-six per cent."

Pye made a note of the figures.

"That's very satisfactory," he said; "and I'm very glad to hear it. I thought the land in one or two places didn't look in too good condition. It's good news that there's to be such notable improvement."

"And, Sir Pye," the official went on, "the changes that have taken place! Before the Revolution the peasants were treated like cattle. Now they have schools, clubs, newspapers. Yes, Sir Pye, newspapers. In this province alone we have one hundred and twenty-eight newspapers."

Pye was making more notes. His doing so inspired the official to make yet greater efforts.

"Not to mention wall newspapers where grievances get voiced. Not to mention school newspapers. We can all of us learn from little ones, is it not?"

Pye agreed.

"Next week there will be a great conference of collective farm shock-workers in Moscow. Comrade Stalin and Comrade Kokoshkin will address the conference."

"It ought to be very interesting," Pye said. "I'll try and get back for it."

"You should, Sir Pye; you should," the official said.

Pye's articles in the great English Liberal newspaper were widely read and widely quoted. Now at last, readers of the articles thought, we know what really is going on in Russia. It's a great comfort to think that there's at least one newspaper left that gives a balanced, objective, unprejudiced account of things; at least one journalist left who can be relied on not to lose his head;

to give us the facts, truth, and leave us to form our own conclusions.

"Thank you," the editor said to Pye on his return, "for a good and useful piece of work."

Pye stumped off in corduroy breeches to await another call to find out if there was anything in something else.

*   *   *   *   *

In most Russian towns there are certain shops whose windows are well stocked with food and clothing. They are called Torgsin shops. People stand outside them in little wistful groups looking at tempting pyramids of fruit; at boots and fur coats tastefully displayed; at butter and white bread and other delicacies that are for them unobtainable. They cannot buy in the shops because only gold or foreign currency is accepted, and most Russians possess neither. Even if they do possess a little gold it is dangerous to disclose the fact. The shops are mostly patronised by foreigners and by Russian Jews who receive remittances from relatives abroad. For the general public, like the special Ogpu stores, and the special Red Army stores, and the special stores for important Communist officials, they are closed shops.

One day an elderly man drove up in a droshky to the main entrance of a Torgsin shop in the centre of Moscow. It was a cold day; and the man seemed to feel the cold. His face was grey and pinched, yet decided. He wore an old blue coat with gold braid round the sleeves. Something strained in his whole bearing; white gums and tight dry skin suggested under-nourishment. He was, like many another in Moscow, starving. Before the Revolution he had been the captain of a small merchant ship. Now he earned a poor living by teaching languages. His friends still called him Captain Andreyev, which he liked because it reminded him of the past when, it seemed to him now, he had been very happy.

He paid the driver of the droshky generously, giving him nearly all the money he had, and, carrying under his arm a large parcel done up in newspaper, went into the shop. People were waiting at the counters to be served, and a long queue was waiting at the pay-desk. Captain Andreyev joined this queue. Everyone in it was holding something; a few foreign currency notes; a gold watch or ornament.

"They say people are taking gold stoppings from their teeth and bringing them here," someone in front of Captain Andreyev whispered to him.

A peasant woman in the queue overheard. "When you're starving," she said, "you've got to do something." Captain Andreyev nodded. He was not one to chatter with casual acquaintances.

The shop smelt of scent; and somewhere a gramophone was playing. In the pay-desk a Jewess; her face heavily powdered and rouged; a grotesque swollen mask, weighed gold; examined currency notes, and paid out Torgsin bonds. By her side sat an expert whom she consulted when she was in doubt. The expert wore rimless pince-nez and had a long straight nose. Captain Andreyev shuddered and fortified himself by looking round at the counters where food was arranged. He and his family had eaten nothing but bread; very little of that, for some months. The Jewess's manner was supercilious. She scarcely liked to touch the articles or the grimy creased notes that were handed to her; picked them up daintily in pincers; spoke only when it was absolutely necessary, and then in insolent monosyllables. Between one customer and another she looked at her pink finger-nails.

An old woman; wizened, bent, a shawl over her head, stood muttering to herself while the Jewess examined a tiny gold coin she had given her. When she handed back the coin and shook her head, the old woman pleaded: "Please take it. It's gold. I know it's gold."

The Jewess ignored her and looked enquiringly at the next in the queue.

"You pig! You devil! You filthy Jew!" the old woman shrieked, her voice cracked and venomous. Then, when she noticed the doorkeeper; an old man in a brown uniform and with a divided beard, move towards her, she slunk out of the shop and joined the little crowd staring at its window display in the street outside.

It was a tragic pawnshop whose goodwill was famine and whose management was terror. It was Ouspenski's promised land adapted to the circumstances of an economic collapse. It was penitents laying capitalist offerings at the feet of the Dictatorship of the Proletariat. The Jewess's swollen face was an idol and the shop a shrine where sacred rites were held; creased, grimy pieces of paper, and gold and jewels, clutched in the fists of the devout, then humbly laid on the shrine. It was Ouspenski's glory and his kingdom.

"I have," Captain Andreyev said when his turn came, "some gold to sell. Rather a lot."

He unwrapped his parcel and displayed the model of a ship; made of gold; each detail perfect; even the name Katya printed in minute letters on its prow. The Jewess half rose from her place; and the expert examined the ship eagerly, taking off his rimless pince-nez and screwing a magnifying glass into his eye.

"You'd better come and see the manager," he said.

The manager was polite. He laughed nervously, and said, "If you don't mind we'll go and see the director. It's a lot of gold. Too much for me to handle."

They drove in a car to see the director, the gold ship on the seat between them. When the car drew up at the headquarters of the Ogpu, Captain Andreyev smiled. "I thought the director probably lived here," he said. An orderly showed them into the commandant's office. He was in uniform; very smart; scented like the Torgsin shop; a dark, quick man whose features seemed to push out of his face and whose body seemed to push out of his uniform. He began to question Captain Andreyev.

"How do you come to have so much gold when you know the Government needs it?"

"I've got papers," Captain Andreyev answered, producing them.

The commandant looked over the papers.

"I see the ship was a presentation."

"Yes, from an American liner. It caught fire; and I was able to be of some service."

"So it appears. In fact, you saved the lives of the crew and passengers."

"Some service," Captain Andreyev muttered.

There was a pause. The commandant seemed to be thinking.

"Why didn't you sell it before?" he suddenly asked.

"I was fond of it. Such a lovely thing. So perfectly made. So accurate. And I liked to have it in my room, and to show it off to people. Besides, it's an exact copy of my own ship that I sailed for twenty years."

"And now?"

Passion swept over Captain Andreyev's face like a wind, twitching his mouth, trembling the corners of his eyes, drawing the skin over his cheekbones.

"Now I need food. My wife and children need food very badly. She persuaded me. But I should have sold it in any case."

An orderly brought in a dossier, and the commandant looked it through quickly.

"I see there has already been a house search and a cross-examination."

"I begged for the ship, and told them it was made of brass and no use to anyone except to me. They let me keep it."

The commandant shut up the dossier and gave Captain Andreyev back his papers.

"You're liable to arrest for having hoarded gold," he said. "Also the gold is liable to confiscation. As a class enemy with bourgeois antecedents you'd get a long sentence if I charged you. In view of the circumstances, however, I shan't charge you; and I shall allow you to have a third of the gold's value in Torgsin bonds."

He smiled patronisingly. Captain Andreyev did not smile back, but bowed stiffly and left the room.

In the afternoon he went back to the Torgsin shop and bought food. He had a curious feeling in buying it that he was spending his soul. There was a chill inside him as he bought; a sense of shame. He felt this very acutely as he walked home through the hungry streets, not because other people were starving and he about to be fed, but because he had sold his gold ship.

He put down the food he had bought without a word, and went out again, leaving his family to eat. They would eat, he knew, shamefacedly and voraciously; conscious that neighbours would have lifted the lids off saucepans in the kitchen to see what was cooking; conscious of people smelling their food and envying them their good fortune; torn between pity and their appetites. Let them eat, he thought; I'm not hungry, and wondered if he would ever be hungry again.

He walked up and down by the river until the early hours of the morning, watching barges and little steamers go by; dark shadows moving silently; a mist over the river which made voices and lights indeterminate; voices and lights drifting by while he tried to forget that he'd sold his gold ship, his soul, to Ouspenski.

*   *   *   *   *

Dr. Dyvov, a dentist, had only one little room to live in and receive his patients and operate on them. He sat in his dental chair in the evenings and slept in it at night. It was domestic furniture as well as scientific apparatus. Fortunately the chair's equipment was easily convertible to domestic uses. The little glass table, whereon stood in business hours an array of steel instruments, served conveniently at other times as a dining-table. The spittoon needed no adaptation; and the chair's neck-rest could be raised or lowered according to whether he wanted to read or rest or eat. His room looked on to a street; and passers-by often laughed at the sight of a dentist enthroned in his own dental chair.

He was a short man with an enormous roll of neck billowing over his collar. His complexion was grey and his eyes melancholy. There was something puzzling about his body. In actual bulk it was small. Yet its outline was plump. This gave him the appearance of a deflated football. Obviously he had once been fat. Now his body was emptied of much of its content without altogether losing its original shape. He lived in the wreckage of his old corpulence like a ruined millionaire living in an empty mansion that had once been full of splendid furniture and servants and fawning guests.

His patients were mostly as poor as himself; and since they paid him in depreciated roubles the amount of food that he could buy with his earnings grew less and less. As time went on, too, the number of his patients decreased. Of two evils, toothache and hunger, the former is the lesser; and in times of famine people are little inclined to spend money on a dentist. Thus he had plenty of time on his hands, which he passed staring out of the window and smoking. To economise cigarettes he would take three or four puffs; then put his cigarette out; then after a while light it again.

Another difficulty was that his supplies of dental material began to run out. He was ingenious at inventing substitutes, and at repairing apparatus that, once broken, he could not replace. When he mixed cement to fill a tooth he only used the exact amount required; and he picked up minute fragments of cotton-wool with his pincers, and shook out drops of tincture of iodine so small that they were almost invisible.

Once a foreigner came to him for treatment; an American, well dressed and friendly, whose face smelt of scented soap. They chatted together while Dr. Dyvov explored his mouth with a mirror and prodded here and here with a pointed scalpel.

"I can only suppose," Dr. Dyvov said, "that times will be better for our children."

The American nodded.

"If not it's a poor lookout," Dr. Dyvov went on.

The American nodded again.

"For my part," Dr. Dyvov said, "I can't see much to live for nowadays."

"Nor I," the American agreed.

"I suppose," Dr. Dyvov said without looking up from mixing a stopping, casually but his voice trembling slightly, "that you buy your food in Torgsin with dollars." Then, not waiting for an answer, he went on eagerly, "Will you buy something for me instead of paying in roubles?"

"If you like," the American said, "I'll pay you in dollars and then you can buy what you like."

The other grew agitated. "Oh no, no," he said, "that wouldn't do at all. It wouldn't do at all for me to buy in Torgsin with dollars. I'd have to explain where I got them from. If you'd buy me (whispering) some sausage and butter and white bread."

The American agreed to pay in kind.

Dr. Dyvov was reckless with materials on the American's last visit, and thanked him for the sausage and loaf of white bread, not profusely, but with feeling. In the evening he drew the blinds to hide his room from the street, and locked the door. His manner was so mysterious that he might have been a conspirator instead of a dentist preparing supper. He boiled water to make tea; laid out the sausage and butter and white bread on the little glass table by his dental chair; sat in the chair and began to eat, turning each bite round in his mouth and drinking glass after glass of tea. When he had finished the food he lit a cigarette, and, adjusting the neck-rest to a convenient height, leant back his head and was at ease.

Being replete turned his thoughts to the past. He remembered how, when he had a tolerable practice in one of the poorer Moscow suburbs, he had played the cornet in an orchestra. His great ambition had been to conduct. He had seen himself, a famous conductor, bowing languidly to enthusiastic audiences. Chief cornet in an amateur orchestra was the nearest he had got to realising this ambition. Lately starvation had made him forget music; even the tunes he knew best; even his ambition to conduct. His soul seemed to have dried up lately. There was no longer any music in it. Music, it seemed to him, no longer existed in the world.

He still had his cornet, unsold as yet; and he took it out and played a few cracked notes. It was stiff from disuse and dusty. He had almost forgotten how to play. His fingers moved clumsily amongst the keys. People passing by in the street outside, and in adjoining rooms, heard with surprise the sound of cracked notes coming from his room, and recognised vaguely tunes they had once known but not heard for many years, and were frightened that such tunes should be played in their neighbourhood.

*   *   *   *   *

Mr. Algernon Vosper (the well-known critic and essayist A. V.) stood on the steps of the Metropole Hotel. He was studying the revolutionary theatre and intended to write a little book on the subject and a few articles on the subject, and to give a few lectures on the subject. He found the revolutionary theatre, as he put it, "abounding with vitality and with ideas." It was, in his view, "very interesting and instructive" and approached life from a new standpoint or slant. These startling opinions were to find expression in his book and articles and lectures. Meanwhile he stood on the steps of the Metropole Hotel, having just finished lunching with a party of Soviet men of letters who, like the revolutionary theatre, were also abounding with vitality and ideas. His immense stomach was insecurely encased in a fur coat. It dominated the steps of the Metropole Hotel as the Belfry Tower dominates Bruges, and was the admiration of all passers-by in the street below. One of these extricated himself from the crowd; climbed up to Mr. Algernon Vosper; delicately, affectionately, reverently, stroked the stomach; then, having paid this tribute to its grandeur, hurried down the steps again and was lost to view.

CHAPTER V
COLOUR STUFF
"Hullo! cretins. Uncle Beastly calling."
—Beachcomber

CHAPTER V
COLOUR STUFF

COOLEY in shirt and trousers; braces very noticeable, listened while his secretary translated the day's newspaper. He was frowsy and unwholesome; and his bedroom smelt of his sleeping body. The secretary read expressionlessly, like a loud-speaker announcing Stock Exchange prices:

> "Comrade Stalin's message to the Ogpu on the occasion of its fifteenth anniversary: 'The flaming sword of the proletariat has for fifteen years protected the workers' State and frustrated the plots of its enemies. Long may it continue to do so. Warmest fraternal greetings to the Ogpu on its fifteenth anniversary.'
> "Comrade Kokoshkin's message: 'Under the triumphant leadership of Comrade Stalin the Five-Year Plan has been completed in four-and-a-quarter years. This sublime achievement has been possible because the Ogpu has kept guard; watched night and day with a million eyes; ceaselessly and valiantly struggled against our enemies. All honour to the Ogpu's fifteen years of glorious service.'
> "Comrade Voroshilov's message . . ."

"No more," Cooley interrupted testily. "I've got the hang of that." Anniversaries! he thought. Always anniversaries! What the hell did the American newspaper reading public care about the fifteenth anniversary of the Ogpu? Worth at most a few lines in some obscure corner. "Why don't they do something instead of celebrating anniversaries?" he said.

The secretary looked up curiously, but said nothing. She was a pale, squat woman with dark anxious eyes. Why don't they do something? her mind echoed; and she saw Cooley leading his forty million readers to rage and destroy across Russia; setting fire to crops and shooting down peasants so that the forty million might have blood to drink and flame to warm themselves; exulting in headlines—"Famine and Terror Stalk the Ukraine." She continued with her reading:

> "Black metallurgy plan ninety-three per cent. fulfilled. The Order of Lenin has been conferred on the Stalin Plant at Gorki . . ."

"Tired of figures," Cooley interrupted. He had often tried to cut a way through the jungle of Soviet statistics, but without success. "Tired of figures," he repeated angrily, pouring whisky into his tooth glass. "You can't make a story out of figures."

The secretary nodded sympathetically.

"And what do they mean," he went on, his voice petulant, "by saying they're going to complete fifteen blast furnaces this year when they're hopelessly behind with last year's schedule? (banging the table). What do they mean by it? I've asked all sorts of people; the Commissar for Heavy Industry himself; but I haven't been able to get a satisfactory reply. It looks as though they're just trying to fool us."

"There's an article in *Isvestia* on using human hair to make felt boots," the secretary said.

Cooley looked up eagerly. He saw possibilities. His mind, a sun with forty million satellites, was stirred and excited by the prospect of making felt boots out of human hair. They might make a pair out of Stalin's hair, he thought; and I might buy them, and show them off in New York, and then sell them as a curio. There was a get-rich-quick element in the idea. Something you thought of, and that became a craze, and that yielded a great harvest of dollars and publicity. Then hair. Any sort of hair. Beard, moustache, under the armpit, in secret places. The idea was salted to the taste of the forty million.

"My, that's better," Cooley said. "Just give me the general drift of that and I'll write a piece."

She explained how the hair was to be collected each day in special vans and stored in special depots, and how the average growth of hair per month per adult, without taking beards into account, would provide sufficient material to make point six of a pair of felt boots, and how all good Soviet citizens would be expected henceforth to grow their hair and beards for the sake of socialist construction. Cooley typed:

> "human hair makes soviet footwear stop todays isvestia contains strong appeal citizens deliver surplus hair special state depots stop new process patented whereby human hair used manufacture felt boots. . . ."

When he had finished he began to walk restlessly up and down the room. "Haven't you heard any gossip?" he asked. "Colour stuff for mailed articles. Human interest. Love affairs of the Kremlin. Commissar and ballerina."

She shook her head.

"This place is dead," he went on, and sat smoking and thinking and drinking whisky out of his tooth glass. " Mrs. Stalin; Mrs. Molotov; Mrs. Kalinin—who are they? Where are they?" he asked.

The secretary knew nothing about them.

Cooley's bed was unmade; pyjamas on the floor; a smell of whisky and tobacco smoke. In shirt and trousers; thick-necked, and with grey cropped hair growing low on his forehead, he strode up and down his stale bedroom demanding colour stuff; human interest stuff; love affairs of the Kremlin; commissar and ballerina.

*   *   *   *   *

In the evening Cooley put on rubber shoes and padded about the streets of Moscow. A pale furtive figure, he too belonged to shadows; rose from mud to stalk angry-eyed through the night with his forty million followers. He moved swiftly and silently about the streets of Moscow looking for food to give to the insatiable forty million; his heavy white face scowling, and his dull eyes longing to tear open bodies and buildings and discover their secrets; looking for death and secret anguish; looking for colour stuff. Cries mocked him; and faces in alley ways, suddenly withdrawn, lured him this way and that like sounds and sweet airs on Caliban's island.

He found nothing because what he sought was everywhere. Misery was too general in Moscow to meet his purpose. Want and death and despair lost their news value in abundance; and, looking for suicide, rape, adultery, murder, any sort of crime or perversion, he groped aimlessly in the darkness of a single crime, a single perversion.

By the Kremlin he paused. There was a story. Each dome and tower a story. Lights coming and going; motor-cars and people passing the sentries, all stories. If only he could find out who they were and what was their business! He padded round the Kremlin wall like a prisoner round the walls of his cell. Was it a shot he heard, and a woman, half undressed, shrieking as she rushed along a corridor? Lenin's mistress shooting a lover. Stalin's wife taking poison. Kalinin's ballerina in a bad temper breaking bottles on his head. Cooley's mouth watered. He saw a front page all his own with photographs and huge black type. Saw it as he padded in rubber shoes round the Kremlin wall. Felt it in his own disordered soul.

He loitered by the stage door of the Opera House. Whose motor-car; sporting model; engine just throbbing? Who inside the motor-car; sallow; immaculate? Commissar or vice-commissar? Karakhan perhaps, waiting to whisk off a favourite? Or was there anyone except Cooley loitering meanly, slyly, by the stage door of the Opera House on the lookout for a story? If I can't get a story, he thought, I might pick up a girl myself. Also a story. Only personal. Of no interest to the forty million. He had dollars in his pocket. Real money. These were power. He could buy anything he liked in Moscow for dollars. "It's all so very, very interesting," he used to say when he lectured to rotary clubs in the United States. Soft lechery, white and puffy like his flesh, inflamed by dollar notes in his pocket, stirred in him.

Not finding a girl, he went back to the Kremlin. They've all got rid of their plain revolutionary wives, he thought; of their Krupskayas; of their tough feminist partners. Now they have smart girls. There must be stories. There must be drama. There must. He remembered a tea party that Lunacharsky gave; the back of the room panelled with a great oil painting of Lunacharsky, and Lunacharsky's wife in black silk; her fingers loaded with rings; her eyes staring out vaguely from deep shadows. Drama, he had called it in his telegram. Real-life drama.

He remembered, too, a reception in the Kremlin in honour of the Soviet-Turkish Treaty. More drama. History being made. The commissars' new wives in their Paris gowns had looked one another over suspiciously; and, as he had telegraphed, the whole assembly was brilliant and glittering and in keeping with the magnificence of its setting. Except for the Tennessee Trial he'd never seen such drama or such history being made. From log-cabin to White House. From Siberian exile to the Kremlin. From underground printing press to the Dictatorship of the Proletariat. Why isn't there some more drama? he thought petulantly as he padded round the Kremlin wall. Why isn't some more history made? A huntsman stalking suicide, rape, adultery, murder.

He saw the headlights of a motor-car moving towards

one of the gateways. Who was in it? Where was it going? A powerful black car with, it seemed to Cooley, the blinds drawn. He stepped forward to look; and the car's lights blinded him, made him glorious and radiant with drama. He fell, transfigured, before the car, and was killed.

* * * * *

The other journalists collected round Cooley's coffin before he was cremated. They were solemn. Poor old Cooley, they thought, and seemed to see his mutilated body; grey stubborn face relaxed; dull eyes cold and still. Jefferson shuddered. Golden youths and maids all must, like chimney sweepers, come to dust. Though you got away with it all your life, and always kept on the side of those who were getting away with it, there came an end. Something got away with you at last. Cooley had finished. How would he finish? Cadging drinks in Paris cafés from patronising ashamed friends. Overgrown senility like Muskett. A home or an asylum or a charitable institution. There's no security nowadays, he fretted once more.

Ouspenski and Mr. Aarons represented the Dictatorship of the Proletariat at the funeral. Their presence gave Cooley's corpse precedence. He jumped up to the top of the queue, and shot to destruction in record time.

"Latest crematorial machinery," Ouspenski whispered proudly.

Mr. Aarons in a black suit, and leaning slightly forwards, expressed his appreciation of the deceased's character, and, in the name of the Dictatorship of the Proletariat, regretted his passing. Oval, sallow, Christ-like face and sparse black beard, occasional tufts of long silky hairs, he fitted the ceremony. He was by nature funereal. Karl Keightan made a little speech. "Coo," he said, "was one of the best. A good pal and a good journalist. He died as I'm sure he'd have wished to die —getting a story."

With a goblet containing Cooley's dust under his arm Ouspenski climped jauntily into an aeroplane. "This is a Soviet plane, gentlemen," he said; "and was manufactured in a Soviet factory out of Soviet materials."

"And Cooley?" Jefferson wanted to ask. "What about him?"

"Following out the instructions of our poor departed friend's relatives," Ouspenski went on, "I propose to scatter his ashes from the air."

In other backward countries, he implied, scattering is done from motor-cars or carts or even wheelbarrows. The Dictatorship of the Proletariat is up-to-date and scatters from the air.

The aeroplane mounted into the sky; and Ouspenski threw Cooley's dust in handfuls down on to Moscow. When he rejoined the others he turned the goblet upside down to show that it was empty; like a conjurer demonstrating the innocence of his apparatus.

Cooley's secretary had one last duty to perform. "cooley cremated scattered today cooley," she typed. He would not, she reflected, have thought it much of a story. Even so, it was news; and he would have approved of sending it in as few words as possible.

*   *   *   *   *

The foreign journalists collected in the Metropole for a drink. They were subdued. Death had come amongst them, and reminded them that they too were material for colour stuff; liable to death, rape, adultery, suicide. The forty million, lacking other food, might make a meal of them. Only Hartshorn looked unusually alert and important. "I have a communication to make," he said when they were alone together, and took a sheet of paper out of his pocket and began to read:

> "Last night just before midnight agents of the Ogpu entered the private house of an English engineer employed in Russia; made an intensive search; confiscated papers, and arrested four Englishmen who are at present detained in Lubianka prison. Forty Russians were also arrested. . . ."

The others had expected something about Cooley. They had thought that perhaps Hartshorn would suggest opening a subscription list for his widow. Their faces were relaxed and generous, and their eyes friendly and indolent. When they realised that it was news; a big story; amazing drama, they started up clamouring, "Tell us more!" their faces stiffened, and their eyes suspicious and narrow. Had Hartshorn, they wondered, stolen a march on them? Had he sent the story off already?

"No, boys," Hartshorn soothed. "I'm playing fair. I'll tell you all I know. It's a matter of principle."

"Poor old Coo," Karl Keightan muttered. "Just the story he was waiting for."

He should have died hereafter.

"Tell us more," the boys clamoured.

What Hartshorn told them formed itself into words in their minds; headlines, then rather smaller type, then little type; dribbled out of their fingers' ends as nervous taps on a typewriter keyboard; became marks on paper. They carried their pieces of paper to Mr. Aarons, who was sitting at home in a short dressing-gown, decorated like a bandsman's tunic, amongst his editions of Marx and Lenin in limp black leather, and his portraits of Marx and Engels and Lenin and Stalin hanging symmetrically one on each wall.

"Gentlemen," he said, flurried, disturbed; "we'll have to go to the Foreign Office. I'll have to consult with my colleagues."

It was one of the occasions on which Mr. Aarons had doubts.

They followed him; still holding their pieces of paper, some of them carrying typewriters. They banged their pieces of paper down on Ouspenski's desk, made statements defining their position, insisted; pleaded. In their dingy waiting-room with its red plush furniture they waited while Ouspenski got his instructions from the Dictatorship of the Proletariat. Their voices made a confused jumble of sound. "With me it's a matter of principle," Hartshorn said. "I've lived by principles all my life."

Carver was more cautious. He was a Soviet citizen and knew what would be, for him, the consequences of a too rigid application of principles. "I don't want to lose my press card," he said. "Besides, Ouspenski's an old friend of mine. We've worked together. We've made love to girls together. We've been drunk together. That makes the position rather different in my case."

Balliger, a little Central European Jew, sat quietly in his place. He had had difficulties before over sending forbidden messages to his newspaper. There had been an interview with Mr. Aarons. "A shocking message," Mr. Aarons had said. "A really shocking message. You! to send such things. You of all people."

(You; one of us; one of the family, he had meant.)

"Shocking but true," Balliger had replied. "It was an official document. I've got the document; and I'll show it to you if you like."

"You've been misinformed," Mr. Aarons had gone on; "and I shall have to ask you to acknowledge the fact in your newspaper. Otherwise you'll be *persona non grata* here." Otherwise, Balliger had thought, I'll have to go away. He had a wife and children, and a living to earn. The two Jews had understood each other perfectly, and wanted to adjust matters in a decent respectable way without any unpleasantness. They had searched about in their minds for a formula that would enable them to make their little deal without hurting each other's feelings. The formula had occurred to both simultaneously. He's got a wife and family. Poor chap! he's got a wife and family. I mustn't make things difficult for him, they had both thought.

"Very well," Balliger had said; "since you've got a wife and family, and since I know you'd get into trouble if I didn't contradict the message, I agree."

"Of course I realise," Mr. Aarons had said, "that

you wouldn't have done it unless you had a wife and family to consider."

They had shaken hands and smiled, satisfied; friendly journalist and Dictatorship of the Proletariat.

Thus, for Balliger, too, it was less a matter of principle than for Hartshorn. "It's a good opportunity for making a protest, don't you think?" he whispered to Rosenfeld, representative of a Jewish news agency. Rosenfeld nodded without enthusiasm. His head was yellow and hairless.

"By the way," Balliger went on, "you don't happen to have any roubles, do you?"

They settled down to an earnest discussion about roubles.

"There's no smoke without fire," Karl Keightan said in a loud voice, wanting Mr. Aarons to hear. He didn't quite like the situation. Obviously the arrested Englishmen had been up to something. Otherwise they wouldn't have been arrested. For instance, he, Karl, had lived for years in Russia without getting arrested. Even so the whole affair was upsetting and difficult to formulate into a straightforward statement of faith. Karl lived by straightforward statements of faith. Arrested Russians were easy to handle. He'd got his formula for them and had used it again and again— "The ways of a revolution are brutal, but direct and perhaps necessary. The sins of the fathers, etc., etc. . . . How easy to destroy, and how painful; how laborious and difficult to create! etc., etc. . . . The old outworn structure of the past falls, and, falling, crushes many whom it sheltered. Yet the foundations of a new and better structure have been truly laid, and storey after storey rises up," etc., etc. . . .

In the present case this formula scarcely applied, and an alternative one was difficult to devise on the spur of the moment. For some months now Karl had been getting anxious about his line. Perhaps I've been long enough on the spot, he thought sometimes. Perhaps it's time to start educating public opinion in the States.

"In my opinion," Jefferson said, "we're kicking the wrong end of the pig."

Ballinger agreed. "After all," he said, "they'll shoot the Russians they've arrested and let the Englishmen go."

"I don't mean that. I mean we're kicking the wrong end of the pig. Approaching the business from the wrong angle," Jefferson said irritably. His mind was running on other matters. He'd been asked to write something about the food shortage, and was trying to put together a thousand words which, if the famine got worse and known outside Russia, would suggest that he'd foreseen and foretold it, but which, if it got better and wasn't known outside Russia, would suggest that all along he'd pooh-poohed the possibility of there being a famine.

He was a little gymnast always balancing himself between two extremes—English gentleman and American newsman; careless Bohemian and Wall Street wiseacre; scholar and smart guy. He trod his tightrope daintily and charmingly. At the very core of his nature there was something fresh and uncorrupt and sensitive; an original goodness which kept him innocent despite the trials and temptations of his circus life.

"Yes, the wrong end of the pig," he said.

"Being back in Moscow has put me right again," Roden said to Muskett.

Muskett rested an arm on his shoulder, like a clergyman when one of his favourite choir-boys says that after all he thinks he'll be confirmed.

"I knew it would," he said. "I knew you'd be all right in the end. I could see you were the sort that would understand. But don't be over-confident. You've got a long and difficult road in front of you."

"This disgraceful business about the arrested engineers makes one ashamed of being English, doesn't it?" Roden went on, anxious to prove the completeness of his cure.

Muskett agreed. Shaking his head he said, "I've often felt ashamed of being English during my ten years in Moscow."

They mourned together for their fallen countrymen.

"In my view," Thicknesse said, "this kind of thing is the worst part of journalism. I like to be able to sit down and figure a thing out. I like to be able to use my mind a bit. Having to hang about here and then dash off what they'll let us send isn't my idea of journalism."

He was a giant with a blond moustache. His mind worked very slowly. When anyone asked him a question his blue eyes grew troubled like an animal's with dumb incoherent suffering. Even drink gave him no sparkle. Only misted over his clear simplicity like hot breath on a window pane. Once in Archangel he had signed an affidavit to the effect that there was no forced labour in Soviet timber camps. All the world was told, "Thicknesse says no forced labour in Soviet timber camps," and was relieved.

"No," he complained, "I like think stuff; and all they want nowadays is colour stuff; sensationalism.'"

The foreign journalists crowded into Ouspenski's room. Mr. Aarons stood by his side. He had forgotten to take off his short dressing-gown decorated like a bandsman's tunic. Ouspenski told them they might send facts without any comment.

"A matter of principle," Hartshorn protested.

"Cut out all my colour stuff!" Thicknesse moaned.

Balliger got Ouspenski by himself and went through his message with him word by word; arguing; suggesting compromises. They were diplomats negotiating a treaty. Old clo' men buying and selling. They enjoyed themselves.

In the end, by one means and another, the World Press got its headlines; and the affair moved on through its inevitable stages.

* * * * *

From time to time the Dictatorship of the Proletariat dramatises its inner conflicts; assembles a cast and plays out on a stage a mimic battle; triumphantly leads itself in chains through the streets of Moscow in honour of a mimic victory. When foreigners figure as principals in such fantastic pageants of self-conflict, the sound and the fury that accompany them gets relayed abroad; and Ouspenski demolishing the fear that is always eating at his heart; fighting his shadow, comes to have a certain substance.

Pye, hurriedly dispatched to Moscow for the occasion, realised at once that everyone else was hysterical, and determined to keep his head. As Mr. Aarons said to him, and as he wrote in the great English Liberal newspaper, "The issue must not be prejudged. These men have been accused of certain things. They may be innocent or they may be guilty. We must await their trial."

Thus he became a property. His glowing pate and walrus moustache figured in the wings while confessions were made and retracted; while witnesses were cross-examined and evidence heard; while speeches were delivered and photographs taken. He was a part of the spectacle; and from within the spectacle he described it with that fairness and impartiality his readers had come to expect of him. Mrs. Eardley-Wheatsheaf thanked God for him. Lord Edderton referred to him in the House of Lords as having vindicated the fair name of British journalism. The Dictatorship of the Proletariat chuckled.

*   *   *   *   *

Mrs. Benson held a salon every Thursday evening. She loved culture, and gathered round her the battered broken fragments of pre-Revolution Moscow intelligentsia along with any first, second or even third secretaries of embassies who would accept her invitations. The battered intelligentsia was somehow apologetic as though it was saying all the time, "Of course we realise that we can be held responsible. But is it after all such a calamity as on first sight it might appear? When all's said and done it *has* meant co-education and birth control clinics and the emancipation of women. And perhaps after a bit, when it's got into its stride, some of the harsher aspects 'll be softened, and there'll be a chance for us again."

They were ancient men and women of letters who used to plead enlightened causes with passionate superiority in reviews long since suppressed, and have discussions and go to concerts, and dream of the day when everyone would own the means of production; and who remained alive now precariously by serving as teachers, and using their eloquence to pour adulation on the head of the Dictatorship of the Proletariat. Their faces were uneasy and tired. Shadowy faces. When they met together in Mrs. Benson's salon they wore shabby old-fashioned clothes; sometimes homespun, that they had saved from before the Revolution, and did their hair in the old ecstatic way, and let their voices fall into the old quick superior accent.

Mrs. Benson moved about her house and amongst her guests like a beetle. She was dark and low built, with swollen indistinct features. The house was old, and in what had formerly been a superior residential suburb. Ceilings hung low over the rooms; passages were dark and musty; little pieces of carpet and cloth were draped here and there on the walls; chairs and tables all covered. It was a muffled ancient house where dust and staleness had long accumulated. Dust lay everywhere. Deposits of dust laid down, stratum after stratum, by successive tenants. Mrs. Benson added her deposit as she moved about the house like a beetle; smiling mouth revealing great fangs of teeth, and breasts quivering under embroidery.

The salon assembled. Dead men and women wearing dead clothes and speaking a dead language crawled into the dead house and came alive in it. They came alive slowly. The house's atmosphere acted on them like artificial respiration. Pharaohs, they opened their eyes, and, finding themselves amongst familiar accoutrements, forgot their thousand mummified years.

Mrs. Benson brought them little cakes and coffee in little cups; and Benson sat in a corner by himself talking steadily; waving short soft fingers in the air as he talked; indifferent whether anyone listened to him or not. A woman with a raw face and little tufts of stiff hair growing on it spoke of a production of the "Cherry Orchard" that she had lately seen at the Art Theatre. "She knew Chekov," the others whispered. "She's going to talk about Chekov. It'll be such an interesting evening."

An atmosphere recreated itself. Fragments of a broken pattern came together for a moment; and the pattern existed again. How nice to gather round one a group of cultivated people! Mrs. Benson thought. She regarded her Moscow salon as a stage towards the achievement of bigger and better salons. Third secretary was eliminated by second, and second by first. In the same way, she hoped, Berlin would follow Moscow, and Paris Berlin, and London Paris, until at last she realised her dream; a salon in New York.

An old lady with grey hair straggling like twilight over a yellow, lined face muttered to herself. Even before the Revolution she had been eccentric. Now she was mad. Her voice grew shrill and argumentative. "I never admit the argument about the organisation of labour. Make the past a *tabula rasa*; no property; no family, and labour will organise itself. You might say that the labour force ought to be studied; its qualities ascertained, and all the rest of it. No such thing. All an utter waste of time. The labour force finds a certain form of activity of itself. Always has. First there were slaves; then . . ."

Her voice quavered away to nothing. The pattern was broken up again. Only Benson went on talking and waving his short soft fingers in the air, and Mrs. Benson moving like a beetle without particular movements. The rest were silent and still.

Tabula rasa, they thought; and heard their own voices speaking twenty years before, and shuddered. *Tabula rasa.* It had come to pass. The slate was clean; and they first of all had been wiped off. The old woman's voice was an echo; the past stalking into Mrs. Benson's salon and reminding them of the present. *Tabula rasa.* Yes, *tabula rasa.* They no longer existed. They were dead. An old man with swollen veins on his hands who was just going to say something about a book he had written found himself dumb. The lady who was reminiscing about Chekov had no more to say. The furtive secondary life that had animated Mrs. Benson's salon flickered out; and her guests departed.

* * * * *

Mrs. Thicknesse and Mrs. Carver, who were friends, generally got up at about eleven o'clock; and most mornings they went to the commission shops. These shops bought up second-hand furniture and clothes and jewellery. The two ladies were on the lookout for bargains; and just now was a very good season since, owing to the famine, people were being forced to sell everything they had. The commission shops, unlike the co-operatives, were admirably stocked. You could pick up an ikon or a picture or a jade necklace or a shawl for a few hundred roubles, which, with the rouble at eighty to the dollar, was next to nothing.

They drove to the shops in a Ford car, and went through one after another; handling things; asking their prices; having carpets laid out for their inspection; weighing precious stones in their hands. Most of the other people in the shops were sellers, not buyers. They had parcels under their arms, and approached the shop attendants diffidently. Since Mrs. Thicknesse and Mrs. Carver were smartly dressed American ladies with money in their pockets they naturally took precedence over the other customers.

Ikons did not attract them much. "You can never tell with ikons," Mrs. Thicknesse said. "Most of them are new and not worth much." Sometimes, however, they picked one up and, as Mrs. Carver said, gave it the once over. A tortured grey Christ with his ribs showing and his mouth twisted; insanely agonised, took their fancy. "I guess I'll bring Bill to have a look at that," Mrs. Carver said. "It might be worth something."

Their shopping was leisurely. There was plenty of time and no competition. Every day, too, more and more things were being brought to the commission shops, and the rouble falling lower and lower. Thus to put off a purchase was probably to get a better bargain.

Mrs. Thicknesse was attracted by an artificial bird in a cage. It wound up, and twittered on its perch, and wagged its little head from side to side. After making sure that there was nothing else that more took her fancy that day she bought it, and took it back with her in her Ford car, and played with it for one or two days, and showed it to her guests.

* * * * *

Jefferson sat working late at night. A shaded lamp isolated him from the rest of the room. He worked quickly and excitedly; pausing occasionally; then hammering harder than ever at his typewriter. The article he was writing was one of a series, "Battlefields Revisited," by famous war correspondents. He'd got his line—the astonishing quickness with which all trace of trenches and battles and bombardments had vanished; flowers growing on, and rabbits burrowing in, land drenched with so much blood; human industry making good in a few years what human folly had destroyed:

"When I stood there and saw how completely the scene was transformed; when I remembered what the place had looked like the last time I had seen it; when I recalled the hundreds of thousands of brave men who had lost their lives and been mutilated in that little patch of land, I marvelled at the power of human beings to repair the consequences of their own folly. The earth, I thought, should have been blood-stained still considering how much blood had been spilt on it; yet it was green and fresh with spring. Buildings, I thought, should be rising out of a wilderness of ruin; everywhere was neatness, husbandry, without a trace of the unbroken desolation I had seen fifteen years before. It was almost shocking that the past should have been so easily and so completely obliterated. I could have found it in me, considering the tendencies, daily stronger, that make for another Armageddon, to wish that the marks of the last had endured a little longer, if only to remind the new generation what their fathers had to suffer and what they will have to suffer if . . ."

He had finished his four-and-a-half sheets. A generous thousand words. He looked them over, satisfied with them. The piece read quite well, he thought. His mind turned back to his life in Paris during the war. It was then that he had first really understood the importance of getting away with things; had realised that description was incomparably less dangerous and more profitable than action. It was then that he had formed his basic impression of the world —a place where men, in their unutterable folly, tore out each other's hearts and probed cruelly into each other's souls; but where an intelligent minority, standing apart, directing, controlling, orating, buying and selling, writing, was able, not merely to be immune from, but even to profit by, these disasters.

He had made up his mind that he must belong to this minority, and so, when the war was over, he had attached himself to the Dictatorship of the Proletariat, which was composed of big boys with big ideas and a big army. He felt safer attached to the skirts of big boys. The bigger they were the better. If one or other for any reason got liquidated or bumped-off, disappeared, Jefferson skilfully detached himself. The big boy of today was not necessarily the big boy of tomorrow. He kept up-to-date in his allegiances. When Bukharin was in favour he was one of the great intellects of the age; when he fell into disgrace he was an opportunist humbug. The first sign of the final collapse of the Dictatorship of the Proletariat will be Jefferson's quietly transferring himself to other skirts, browsing in other pastures.

CHAPTER VI
DIPLOMATIC INCIDENT

"L'historien officiel de l'Empire des Tsars, Karamsine, a raconté comment Boris Godounof s'y prenait déjà pour cacher aux ambassadeurs étrangers l'état de la Russie. 'Depuis les frontières jusqu'à Moscou, il les environnait d'une abondance et d'un luxe apparents; ils voyaient sur leur passage des gens richement vêtus, les marchés etaient remplis de toutes sortes de denrées, et pas un seul mendiant ne s'offrait à leur vue, lorsque, à une verste de là, les tombeaux s'encombraient de victimes de la faim.' "—HENRY ROLLIN

"Ce goût du secret a d'ailleurs une origine fort ancienne et dans son 'Journal du voyage des Ambassadeurs de Holstein en Moscovie et en Perse,' Oléarius, qui séjourna en Russie de 1633 à 1637, raconte qu'au bout de quelque temps on leur permit de visiter les ambassadeurs de Suède.... Oléarius voyait là un grand progrès car 'cy-devant on enfermoit les ambassadeurs étrangers et leurs gens dans le logis, on les gardoit comme des prisonniers et l'on mettoit des corps de garde aux portes pour les empescher de sortir, ou, si on permettoit a leurs gens de sortir, on les faisoit accompagner de strelitz qui observoient toutes leurs actions.' "—HENRY ROLLIN

"The official historian of the Empire of the Tsars, Karamsine, told how Boris Godunov took it upon himself to hide from foreign ambassadors the condition of Russia. 'From the frontiers to Moscow, he surrounded them with abundance and apparent luxury; on their trip they saw richly dressed people, markets were full of all sorts of products, and not one beggar was offered to their sight, when, less than a mile from there, the graves were filled with victims of hunger.' " — HENRY ROLLIN

"Moreover, this taste for secrecy had an exceedingly old origin, and in his 'Journal of the Trip of Some Ambassadors from Holstein in Moscow and in Persia,' Olearius, who resided in Russia from 1633 to 1637, told that at the end of some time they were permitted to visit the ambassadors from Sweden. . . . Olearius saw great progress there because 'formerly the foreign ambassadors and their people were locked up in the house, were guarded like prisoners, and a company of guards was placed at the doors in order to prevent them from going out, or, if their people were permitted to go out, they were accompanied by soldiers who watched all their actions.' " — HENRY ROLLIN

CHAPTER VI
DIPLOMATIC INCIDENT

THE Andulasian Ambassador walked up and down his large room in the Andulasian Embassy. He was middle-aged and inclined to be stout. Grey hair trimmed a yellow pate; and teeth, noticeably false, gleamed underneath a grey moustache. Time had coated him with layers of indolence; belly with fat; eyes with a bilious mist; skin with dry pouches. The years he had spent in Moscow had laid down the heaviest deposit of all; and when he looked back on his life before he came there, he saw it indistinctly through a fog of indolence. Now, however, a diplomatic incident had arisen whose effect on him was like a spring-cleaning in a neglected office—clouds of dust rising from carpets; forgotten corners stirred up; accumulated papers shifted; an established peaceful disorder changed into an active disorder.

He had received that day a letter informing him that Insnab, the special shop for diplomats, was to be closed, and that henceforth he would have to buy his provisions at Torgsin with foreign currency. This was a serious matter. It considerably increased his living expenses; and, he thought, the insolence of it! A letter from a grocer! Who is Torgsin? I have no official knowledge of him. I refuse to accept the communication. He rang his bell for a secretary and gave orders that the letter should be filed under "Miscellaneous circulars: not to be answered." That'll teach 'em, he thought; then, too agitated to play his customary morning game of billiards, he settled down to write a long dispatch to his Government about the whole affair.

The Ambassador had come to Moscow as a result of a Liberal revolution in Andulasia. His uncle had been one of the leading figures in the revolution, and, becoming Foreign Secretary in the new Government, had distributed diplomatic appointments to deserving relatives. "Too long," he had said, when announcing his nephew's appointment to Moscow in the newly elected Liberal Legislature, " has this country pursued a policy of unreasonable antagonism in regard to the Soviet Republic. We propose henceforth to aim, not, as our predecessors, at discrediting, but at co-operating with the Government of that great country where such interesting and momentous experiments are being made." The announcement was received by the Liberal deputies, nearly all of whom were lawyers or journalists or university lecturers, with enthusiasm only tempered by the thought that they might have been able to achieve this excellent object even more adequately than the Foreign Secretary's nephew.

Thus the Ambassador had arrived in Moscow with, as he put it himself to the Commissar for Foreign Affairs, an ardent republican heart beating underneath his diplomatic uniform. He studied the Russian language and Soviet institutions with praiseworthy thoroughness; embodied the results of his studies in informative dispatches to his Government, and generally behaved in an exemplary manner. Gradually, however, his enthusiasm evaporated. Apart from his natural indolence, which tended to reassert itself, he found that his dispatches met with no response, and suspected that they were unread; that he was surrounded by spies and, as far as he could judge, aimless intrigues; that, apart from ceremonial occasions, Russians, particularly those in important positions, shunned his company; and when, in consequence of a military coup, his uncle retired from public life, and only just managed, with the aid of an aeroplane, to escape retiring from private life too, he finally reconciled himself to living quietly within the confines of his embassy and the small circle of his fellow diplomats.

He played billiards all the year round; tennis in the summer, and skated in the winter. His only intellectual exercise was to attempt to tell someone about a plan he had thought out for solving the unemployment problem. Since he never succeeded in making himself understood the exercise proved inexhaustible. His only relations with the Dictatorship of the Proletariat were an occasional reception at the Foreign Office or a game of poker with the *chef-du-protocol*, who almost invariably won. Sometimes he tried to pull the Dictatorship of the Proletariat's leg by writing on a piece of paper, "Pay Mr. Aarons five hundred dollars for services rendered," and leaving it about in the hope that one of the many Ogpu agents in the Embassy would find it. Except for the fact that his salary continued to be paid there seemed no reason to suppose that his Government had not quite forgotten his existence; and until another

Liberal revolution took place he thought it wiser to refrain from pushing himself into notice.

When he had finished his dispatch and arranged for it to be sent *au clair* ("I want 'em to know what I've written," he said to Lopaz; a young man with a pointed head and a large nose, who held pronounced anti-Semitic views. "It'll do 'em good. Not that they wouldn't know if I sent it in code; but they might miss some of the sarcasm if we left 'em to decode themselves") he again walked up and down his room, planning out the crushing remarks he would make to Soviet officials when he happened to meet them. "Supposing, M. le chef-du-protocol," he would say with icy politeness; bowing so; casually lighting a cigarette so, "you do me the honour to ask me to sit down to cards, may I know whether the stakes are to be in roubles or dollars or pounds or what?" The *chef-du-protocol*, who was after all a gentleman, if a shady and decayed one, would, he hoped, be overcome with confusion.

In the afternoon the Ambassador called by appointment at the Foreign Office. He had dressed himself carefully in a morning coat and top hat and silk socks and button boots with suede tops. His moustache was waxed, and his face wore, he hoped, an expression of gay, careless inscrutability. The Commissar for Foreign Affairs looked at him amiably through square spectacles; face round and serene; little plump fingers drumming on the desk at which he sat. Once, the Ambassador recollected, his name had been Harris; and he was tempted to make a slip and begin by addressing him as Monsieur 'Arris.

"I received this morning," the Ambassador said, " a sort of circular from a grocery establishment. Would you be so kind as to explain what it means?"

This, tilting one eyebrow and with a suspicion of a smile. The effect was spoilt by its too fleshy setting; like a fat clown doing acrobatics. The eyebrow moved ponderously, and the suspicion of a smile turned into a smirk.

"You refer perhaps," the Commissar for Foreign Affairs said, "to the privilege it has been decided to extend to foreigners whereby they are allowed to use their own currency without changing it into roubles."

They fenced together for half an hour or so. At the end, as he took his leave, the Ambassador said with some heat: "I've done my best to be friendly during my time in Moscow. I've overlooked a great deal, and have always been ready, if you wanted it (which you didn't) to help with advice; in more practical ways when questions affecting our two countries arose. During the negotiations for a Soviet-Andulasian non-aggression pact you never once came near me. I didn't complain; though, I might remind you, the negotiations proved abortive. Now you have taken this step without any warning or previous consultation. Just sent me a printed circular from a grocer. Coupled insolence with robbery. My Government has been fully informed of so flagrant an infringement of diplomatic usage; and I can assure you that the matter will not be allowed to rest where it is." He bowed; and the Commissar for Foreign Affairs eagerly held out his hand.

"The relations between our two countries remain

friendly," he said; his voice eager, conciliatory; like a greengrocer with a guilty conscience when a customer has made a complaint about a delivery of inferior potatoes—" We'll continue to have your custom, I trust?"

"That remains to be seen," the Ambassador answered, "and depends on what action, if any, you intend to take to remedy the existing situation."

A great deal had gone on while the Ambassador was playing billiards in his Embassy, or was trying to explain his scheme for solving the unemployment problem; and while the Commissar for Foreign Affairs was sitting at his desk and dreaming of non-aggression pacts. A great deal had gone on that both found it more convenient to ignore. They played billiards and dreamed while terror and death danced round them. Like peasants living under the shadow of Etna, they forgot at their billiards and dreaming the crater overflowing with fiery destruction. Like old men drowsing in clubs over newspapers containing accounts of ferocious battles won and lost, they shot little balls into pockets and fashioned the clauses of treaties while a space was relentlessly cleared to make room for Ouspenski's promised land.

Driving back to the Embassy the Ambassador noticed an old woman lying on the footpath. People passing up and down the street stepped over her as though she had been a stone or a heap of garbage. No one looked at her face or moved her aside. Snow was gently piling up on her. It looked as though soon she would be quite covered. The Ambassador remembered his conversation with the Commissar for Foreign

Affairs; its substance, its character, and felt sick, and understood. He ought to explain. He ought to send dispatches, even if no one read them, describing this fearful reality. Why should he too pretend? Why? For a moment he stood apart and understood. Even in Andulasia the swindle was less barefaced; less pretentious. Like Tchounikine he wanted to protest—as a civilised South American; as a man; an animal, genus *homo sapiens*, forked radish. Standing feet astride in front of the Embassy fireplace, Mr. Aarons had said, "You must admit that we look after the very young and the very old. You must at least give us credit for having spread education." He had admitted and given credit. He had lived within the swindle. Now he stood apart.

He stopped his car. The little flag on the front hurried on passers-by. He tried to lift up the old woman; her complexion grey; her head lolling. I'll lose the confidence of my Government, he thought. I'll be attacked in the Press. Hysterical. Absurd. A young man in a black leather coat officially interfered, murmuring tenderly, "*Babashka; babashka.*" A policeman, taking his cue from the young man in the black leather coat, approached and also murmured tenderly, "*Babashka; babashka.*" Soon a little crowd was chanting, "*Babashka*; *babashka*. Poor dear old granny."

"We'll take her to the Lenin Home for Aged Workers," the young man said. "Or to the Stalin Institute for Proletarians of Riper Years."

"It's too late," the Ambassador said severely as he got back into his car. "She's dead."

*   *   *   *   *

As the door closed behind the Andulasian Ambassador the Commissar for Foreign Affairs sighed. Other ambassadors would come; one after the other; a procession of ambassadors; all the ambassadors in Moscow except the Persian Ambassador, who had been instructed to be confined to bed with influenza, and the Turkish Ambassador, whose natural good sense would confine him to bed, and the Alsatian Ambassador, who would be too busy to make any visits to anyone that day.

The Alsatian Ambassador was buying heavily in Insnab. He was determined not to waste precious time on diplomatic protests that could be spent more profitably in making rouble purchases. The next day, when the shop was actually closed, would be a more suitable occasion for protesting against the new arrangement than while it was still open. With the vigour and pertinacity that characterise his race he fought his way from counter to counter; his first secretary on one side of him and his second secretary on the other. The shop was crowded and was doing a roaring business. Many others, like the Alsatian Ambassador, had decided to make the maximum use of the single day's grace allowed before Insnab became Torgsin. By closing time the shop was as empty as a garden after being attacked by a flight of locusts. Everything it contained had been bought. The Alsatian Ambassador, sweating and exhausted, climbed into his car. The secretaries climbed into theirs. Both cars were full with the purchases they had made.

For the Alsatian Embassy the change from Insnab

to Torgsin was more serious even than for the Andulasian Embassy. It not merely increased living expenses but robbed the Embassy of its chief source of income. By buying in Insnab and retailing on the open market the Embassy had been able substantially to supplement the meagre and irregular revenue it received from the Alsatian Government, and to keep up decent standards of hospitality and ceremonial. Henceforth, except for inconsiderable profits made from trafficking in roubles, the Alsatian Ambassador would be entirely dependent on his salary. It was not an agreeable prospect; and he was ready now to make any number of diplomatic protests.

* * * * *

That evening there was a great dinner party at the Andulasian Embassy. "We must act together," the Ambassador said over cocktails. Every evening alcohol brightened him up like sun breaking through an autumn mist.

"I quite agree," the Bosnian Ambassador answered, screwing up his mouth. "What shall we do?"

"A joint protest," the Ambassador said. "Something emphatic; unanimous, that they can't ignore."

"Supposing they ask us," the Perugian Ambassador said, bald and rubicund and already slightly tipsy, "where we get our roubles from?"

"I shall answer," the Ambassador said, "that it's no business of theirs."

"Indeed it's not," everyone echoed.

"Well, they know we don't get them from the State

Bank," the Perugian Ambassador went on. "By the way, where do you get yours?"

Everyone looked on the ground. There was an awkward pause. "I believe dinner's served," the Ambassador said.

Between one course and another and between one glass of wine and another they laid their plans. The Ambassador expanded as the dinner proceeded. His spirit filled out the empty spaces in his body like air filling out a football. He became compact and substantial. "Something emphatic and unanimous," he repeated. "They mustn't be allowed to think they can do what they like. We've put up with too much already. It's time we made a stand; and I may tell you in the strictest confidence that I've received authorisation from my Government this evening to act as I think fit in the matter."

"For me," the Simoan Ambassador said, "the situation's rather more complicated. At the moment, as you probably know, trade negotiations are pending . . ."

"The firmer we are," the Ambassador sternly interrupted, "the more likely we are to get satisfaction. If we're weak and divided they'll go on; make us pay for petrol and travelling in gold; even rents."

"He's right," the others agreed. "Quite right."

"For my part," the Ambassador said, "I've made up my mind not to yield an inch."

They moved from the dinner-table to play cards; ladies and gentlemen in evening dress, heavy with food and drink, like cows clumsily moving from one pasture to another. A curious company to find in that place.

A curious little world to exist within that other world. The Ambassador drew the Perugian Ambassador aside. "Supposing," he said, "you let people pay taxes in goods; motor-car manufacturers in motor-cars; brewers in beer. You see what I mean? Then you distributed the goods amongst the unemployed instead of the dole on the condition that they made use of them—drove the motor-cars so many miles; drank so much of the beer, and so on. You see what I mean? The effect would be, wouldn't it? . . ."

The Perugian Ambassador seemed to be listening. His eyes were open. His breathing was regular. His hands were folded in his lap. Really, however, he was asleep.

In due course the united protest was made. The Andulasian Ambassador delivered it himself. "I'll see what can be done," the Commissar for Foreign Affairs said, and put the protest away in a drawer in his desk. In the Andulasian Legislature a member asked the Secretary of State for Foreign Affairs whether he was aware that the Republic's representative in Moscow had been forbidden to use the currency of the country, and that thereby accepted diplomatic usage had been flouted. He was told that the Andulasian Government knew of this situation; was following it carefully, and was taking suitable steps. The *Andulasian Guardian*, a Liberal organ, pointed out that the protest made in the Legislature was not altogether just, since there was reason to suppose that members of the diplomatic corps in Moscow were in the habit of obtaining roubles by illicit means. "Therefore," the *Andulasian Guardian* went on, "we think that all fair-minded, reasonable people, without, on the one hand, refusing to recognise the legitimate grievances of our Ambassador in Moscow, or, on the other, falling a prey to the passions and prejudices with which any question involving the Soviet is fraught, should aim rather at finding a just compromise which will enable both countries to escape without loss of prestige from the present impasse than at fomenting bad feeling which hot-heads, here as well as in Moscow, are only too ready to turn to account."

The united protest was soon forgotten. The Persian Ambassador recovered from his influenza; and the Turkish Ambassador rose from his bed; and the Alsatian Ambassador took steps to extend his rouble-changing business. As he went in off the red the Andulasian Ambassador thought to himself, I showed them they couldn't do what they liked with me at least. I showed them. The mood which had come to him on his way back from his talk with the Commissar for Foreign Affairs had soon passed. After all he had not lost the confidence of his Government or been attacked in the Press. Like Pye, he had avoided being hysterical or absurd.

* * * * *

Lopaz called at the Albanian Consulate. Three men, the Consul and two friends, were sitting together; drinking coffee and chatting. There was a curious impassivity about them as though beneath the surface of their chatter they were asleep or brooding. They gave an impression of stability; a composite statue;

figures arranged once and for all in an unchangeable pattern. Lopaz found himself sitting amongst them. They were round him, shadowy, terrifying, shutting out the light and all hope of escape. He put his hand over his breast pocket where he kept his money and waited for them to address him.

Insensibly, without his noticing when, they changed from speaking Albanian to speaking French. "You've been on leave?" one of them said. "I hear your Ambassador's taken a strong line about the Insnab affair," another said. "The snow's come early this year," the last said. Lopaz answered them separately, turning from one to the other, apprehensive. He was anxious to get away and so came straight to his business. "Can you let me have some roubles?" he asked.

In the kitchen someone was cooking. There was a smell of garlic and a sound of frying. Lopaz saw through the half-opened door a girl moving backwards and forwards. She was squat and dark, and wearing a red dress; a thick-set peasant girl; slow in her movements, and healthy and strong. He wished he might call at the Consulate one day when the Albanians were out. Are they ever out? he wondered. It seemed unlikely.

His question stirred the Albanians. Not actively. In the same way that wind stirs a mountain peak, making it seem, with all its solidity, tremulous and angry. They looked at him enquiringly as though to ask, "Roubles? What in the world led you to suppose that we should have roubles?"

The Consul was huge. His belly hung over his chair;

and the little coffee cup lifted to his face was like a white butterfly fluttering round an immense rock. The other two were small; their faces wizened and screwed up, glossy black curls pasted over sallow brows. "For some reason," the Consul said, "they're difficult to come by just now." It was a routine. Lopaz was not perturbed.

"I'd be most grateful if you could oblige," he said.

"What rate were you thinking of?" one of the little Albanians asked, his head on one side.

"I heard that the Japanese were getting eighty to the dollar."

The Consul laughed quietly in a surprised, complacent way.

"I wish they'd get me some at that rate," he said.

There was a pause. Only the sound of frying in the kitchen disturbed the room's stillness. The three Albanians seemed to solidify again. The wind raised by the first mention of roubles dropped; and their impassivity was by contrast more absolute than before. "If you could manage seventy-five I'd be quite satisfied," Lopaz said timidly. Then, finding the offer met with no response, "Or even seventy."

The three Albanians looked at one another. Without saying anything they consulted together. Their wordless debate took some little time and ended in agreement. "Perhaps we might manage sixty-five," the Consul said.

"It's a poor rate," Lopaz muttered.

He felt their eyes on him, following the movement of his hand as it went to his breast-pocket; the movement of his moistened forefinger as it bent back the corners of dollar bills, and of his arm as it passed them across to the Consul. The Albanians counted out roubles jointly; no particular hand touching them; no particular tongue chanting numbers. Lopaz wrapped his roubles up in a newspaper; a heap of tattered pieces of paper; some fresh and some stale; some from Warsaw and some from Harbin, and sat a little longer in the room. Its heavy warm air made him drowsy. With his newspaper parcel of roubles under his arm he said good-bye to the Albanians, and then hurried home through the biting cold of a Moscow winter's morning.

* * * * *

Ivanov was a bank clerk. He sat at a table some way back from a public counter with an abacus beside him and made additions in a ledger. When, as quite often happened, other clerks shouted questions at him, he would look up from his ledger and, keeping the last total in his mind, try to answer them. He wore spectacles with unusually powerful lenses, and had dark thin hair and high cheek-bones and an anxious, timid mouth. His fingers were slender and supple, and his movements graceful despite his shy manner; like an exquisite body in ill-fitting clothes.

No one knew anything about him; where he came from; who his parents were; what had been his status before the Revolution; even how old he was or whether he was married and had any children. He belonged to the relatively large number of Soviet citizens whose papers had got lost or destroyed, and who had, in a documentary sense, been born again when the Dictatorship of the Proletariat established itself. Since he was a hard-working, quiet, law-abiding person who made few demands on the State and served it faithfully, the Dictatorship of the Proletariat was content to take him for granted and to refrain from asking questions about his social and political antecedents.

Ivanov also had forgotten the past. At least if he sometimes remembered it (another world than the State Bank and his little room on the outskirts of Moscow; hours spent in crowded trams going from one to the other; long waits in queues; pockets stuffed with innumerable documents explaining who he was and where he worked, what trade union he belonged to, each with its lugubrious snapshot attached), it was dimly and objectively, like something he had once seen; a memory of a previous incarnation; centuries, ages ago when life was different in its very nature.

One day to his great surprise and consternation he found on his desk a card inviting him to tea at the Japanese Embassy. Tears filled his eyes, and with trembling fingers he told over the beads of his abacus. Whether he ignored the invitation or whether he accepted it there was only trouble ahead. He had shunned the company of foreigners and lived so discreetly that the Dictatorship of the Proletariat was scarcely aware of his existence. Now, through no fault of his own, he found himself associated, not merely with foreigners, but with a foreign embassy. It was as though a monk had suddenly found a plump harlot in bed beside him, or as though a Nonconformist minister's lips formed, instead of a prayer, a bawdy rhyme.

There was only one thing to do. With the card in his pocket he presented himself at the Foreign Office, and, after some delay, managed to get admitted to the presence of an official. "Look at this!" he said, producing the card like a bomb or a phial of deadly poison. "Look at this!"

The official, head shaven; beard tapering to a fine point, examined the card. "Well?" he asked.

"I don't know how it came to me," Ivanov went on. "I don't know anything about it."

His despair was pitiable.

"Are you going to accept or decline this kind invitation?" the official asked.

"I've come to you for advice."

Ivanov spread out his hands.

"Which is better?"

The official seemed to be thinking aloud. "If you decline," he said, "then obviously you must have previous dealings with foreigners on your conscience. If you accept, then any leakage of information about, say, State finance, will be easy to account for. On the whole, I should say that the less dangerous course would be to accept. Yes, I think you'd better accept."

Ivanov put the card back sadly in his pocket and went home.

On his way to the Japanese Embassy he felt curiously excited. Perhaps knowing that whatever he did trouble was certain, had made him desperate; broken down reserves, habits of caution. He strode along proudly, feeling himself superior to the shabby, gloomy people all round him; feeling that he belonged to a more orderly, more balanced civilisation than they did. Slogans pasted on the outsides of buildings filled him with contempt; and he suddenly realised how dreary his days in Moscow were. Stale, flat and unprofitable, he thought. Empty of everything I care for; of everything worth caring for. He hated even the fantastic towers, delicate and irrelevant, and the golden domes of the Kremlin because they, too, like the slogans, were abstractions; separate from people; fanciful cruel dreams; rootless and fabulous. Too fabulous, he thought, to be satisfying. Too fabulous to be beautiful. Too fabulous. He felt in himself a power of resistance, and knew that he was strong enough to suffer with dignity. He felt at ease and unafraid for the first time since he could remember.

The Japanese Ambassador, surrounded by his staff, received Ivanov with queer stiff formality. Everyone made little stiff bows; and Ivanov began to remember not only a language and a mode of behaviour, but particular scenes; a white courtyard and a fountain playing; cool empty rooms whose light was pale and whose shape serene; quick silent movements over polished floors.

"It took us a long time to find you," the Japanese Ambassador said deferentially. He was a small man with grey hair and a tired face. His morning coat made him look like a blackbird.

"I suppose so," Ivanov answered in Japanese.

"When your father, the Emperor, died," the Ambassador went on, "your mother insisted on returning to Russia. We did our best to dissuade her; but she said that she wanted you to grow up in Russia. After the Revolution we lost all trace of her."

Ivanov was excited. Excitement made his words quick and intense. "She had a lover. A rich man. A merchant. I remember now. When he was shot they sent her away; and I heard long afterwards that she was dead."

It was difficult to tell whether he was smiling or grimacing. His lips were drawn back, exposing white, regular teeth.

"She was," the Ambassador said, "an enchanting dancer, and the Emperor's favourite mistress. We all had a very high opinion of her."

"I never saw her dance," Ivanov said sadly.

He went with the Ambassador into an inner room, where they had tea.

The next day the Ambassador paid a visit to the Foreign Office. He stayed a long time; and his Russian chauffeur, waiting in the road outside, cursed with impatience. When at last he emerged he left the official, with whom he had been, nervously chewing a pencil and fingering papers. As far as he was concerned, however, there was no trace of strain. He trod downstairs as daintily and precisely as he had climbed up; and when he got back to the Japanese Embassy he sent Ivanov a respectful note informing him that his passport was now available. This passport enabled Ivanov to leave Moscow. He left the very same evening for Tokio.

CHAPTER VII
WHO WHOM?

"At bottom, the question of control is really the question: Who is it that exercises control? That is to say, what class controls and what class is controlled?"

— Lenin

CHAPTER VII

WHO WHOM?

WRAITHBY gave a party before leaving London for Russia. He was a dim, fitful person. Floating loose on society; making little darts, like a bee in search of honey, at newspaper offices and literature and politics and love affairs, and then hastily withdrawing into himself; interested in the world and in human affairs but having no contact with either; carried this way and that by changing emotions and convictions, he had observed from afar the Dictatorship of the Proletariat, and had felt it to be substantial. He knew that it was brutal and intolerant and ruthless. He had no illusions about its consequences to individuals and to classes. Only, he thought, it offered a way of escape from himself. It was *Brahma*; an infinite; and by becoming one with it he would cease to be finite. It would relieve him of the burden of his appetites and opinions, and give him peace and humility. It would make it unnecessary for him to formulate points of view about pictures and books and social problems and relationships. His tired mind, everlastingly grinding into his soul like a dentist's drill into a tooth, would be able to sleep on its bosom. It was a sea that would cradle him. A baptism and a rebirth. He longed to lose himself in the Dictatorship of the Proletariat as Lawrence longed to lose himself in the loves of gamekeepers and gipsies.

The last party, he thought. The very last. His friends came to say good-bye to him. Girls with fringes and high-waisted dresses; voices heard on the wireless; names seen in newspapers and periodicals; heads that often floated, like coloured balloons, over platforms at lectures and meetings. They all came, and drank and chattered. Wraithby went from one to the other asking himself Lenin's famous question—Who whom? Who lectured to whom? Who edited whom? Who canvassed for whom? Who voted for whom? Who slept with whom? Who paid whom? Who was whom?

Of Wraithby they all said, "Dear old Wraith! He'll never do anything. How nice he is though!" They meant he was whom. Eternally whom. "Ramsay MacDonald," they all said, "is vain and deceitful and stupid." They meant he was who; they remaining, in relation to him, whom. To the Dictatorship of the Proletariat, they drank. To Ramsay MacDonald over the water, Wraithby thought. "How we envy you, Wraith!" they said.

He smiled and answered, "I'm a coward. It's flight."

"Flight from what and from whom," they asked in chorus.

"From you," he answered.

They laughed. "From us? On the contrary, you're flying to us."

"Are you the Dictatorship of the Proletariat then?" he asked incredulously.

"Of course," they exulted, dancing round him. "Of course."

"I thought," he said, sighing, "that the Dictatorship

of the Proletariat had destroyed us. I thought it was flame that had burnt us up. I thought it was a sun whose rays had blinded us."

Wraithby was drunk. Everyone was drunk except Cavendish, whose lips rolled and quivered over his beard, and whose appetites lived, restless, in his eyes. "Anyway," Wraithby said, "for tonight, Who whom?" He put out the light. There was a rustle of people moving together. Cavendish breathed heavily in his corner; a religious; a philosopher; a visionary.

In the morning Wraithby found himself alone in his room. He drew the blinds, and grey light revealed cushions and empty glasses spread about here and there. In the grate a heap of cigarette ends. So much debris I've accumulated, he thought, and gladly turned his back on it. Carrying two suitcases, one in each hand, he walked along empty London streets, and watched bottles of milk and newspapers being distributed to silent houses.

* * * * *

They were all on the boat. A little longer, Wraithby thought, and they'll be gone; and I'll never see them again. They've come to see me off. When a bell rang, and visitors began to leave, and they remained, he was frightened.

"Hadn't you better be going now?" he said.

They laughed. "Going? We're not going. We're coming with you." Then, noticing his pained surprise, "Only for a trip. Only for a fortnight."

Girls with high-waisted dresses roamed about the

boat as it drifted down the Thames; and everywhere there was a smell of tweeds. "Anyway," Wraithby said, "for the journey, Who whom?" He took the arm of a Girton girl named Anne.

Cavendish stood in the centre of a little group, arms folded, face meditative. He pointed to London. "Look! great buildings; wealth; the heart of a mighty Empire; yet all built on sand; decaying; and this little ship flying a red flag creeping into the heart of it like a male sperm fertilising an ovum; the future finding its way into the past; life finding its way into death." He waved them away. "I want to be alone," he said.

They tiptoed off, awed and respectful. "He understands," they whispered. "But how few do!"

The crew entertained the passengers by singing revolutionary songs. They cut their revolutionary capers and did their revolutionary tricks. Already the curtain was up and the play begun. The passengers reciprocated with a tableau. It ought, they thought, to be decently godless so as not to offend the crew's susceptibilities, and, at the same time, to indicate that this particular set of passengers appreciated, and were largely in sympathy with, the Dictatorship of the Proletariat. They decided on a tableau of the creation. Cavendish was God. He sat, benign, amongst his creatures. Wraithby was Adam, and Mrs. Trivet, in a backless bathing costume, Eve. Mr. Trivet was the serpent, and Lord Edderton an angel. Cavendish made a speech that was translated into Russian. "You," he said, turning to Adam and Eve, "have sinned. Your reward is that you will be allowed to leave this drearily perfect

Garden of Eden and to go to a world that needs to be perfected. Yours the joy of perfecting and populating the environment in which I shall place you. Yours the privilege of centuries of struggle. Yours the ecstasy of discovery and achievement. Yours the final triumph in the realisation of a classless socialist society. Meanwhile, take this and be happy!" He handed them a contraceptive. Everyone laughed. He was a glib, eloquent man; a Member of Parliament, a left-winger famous for his passionate sincerity. The head steward, commenting on the tableau in a long speech, said that he regretted that no mention had been made of the Five-Year Plan. Cavendish, in a gay rejoinder, admitted the fault, but pleaded that he had, consciously and deliberately, confined himself to generalities. "You see," he whispered to Lord Edderton, "how everything is open to discussion. Everyone is free to criticise. Can you imagine it happening on a P. and O. boat?" Lord Edderton said that he could not imagine it happening on a P. and O. boat.

When the discussion was over Wraithby carried Mrs. Trivet off to her cabin. He staggered under her weight; and her flesh divided on each side of his shoulder like a sack of flour. In the cabin she took his face in her hands and whispered, "My fairy man! My fairy man!" Then, "You're unhappy. Let love restore you. Let love purify you. Let me magic you." She reached for him. He felt himself falling into a bottomless well; drowning in a troubled sea of flesh; choking and suffocating as wave after wave of flesh washed over him.

The boat sailed past Kronstadt in the early morning.

Wraithby found a group of third-class passengers in the prow. He had not noticed them before. They had taken no part in the revolutionary songs or the tableau, but had hidden all through the voyage in some corner of their own. Most of them were Russians who, after starving in Paris or London or New York, were returning to Russia. Kronstadt was their first glimpse of Russia for many years. As they looked at it; ruined fortresses; derelict buildings; all desolate and neglected, their eyes filled with tears. Their mood infected Wraithby. He felt indescribably melancholy as he sailed past Kronstadt. The ruin and desolation of the place filled him with foreboding.

One of the returning exiles, a stocky impassive man, began to dance. There was no gaiety in his movements. They were perfectly regular, yet ecstatic and fiendish. Their ferocious rhythm, beating on the deck like a tom-tom, forced its way into Wraithby's soul. Like the others, he clapped to the rhythm, and, as he clapped, felt despair and a kind of exhilaration sweep through him. After all, the dance was real. It was an expression of something and not, like the revolutionary songs, the tableau, Mrs. Trivet's magic, dust floating on sunlight. The rhythm became more and more frantic; then stopped; and the dancer was still. The group of third-class passengers remained in the prow until Kronstadt was out of sight.

Just before the boat reached Leningrad the captain delivered a lecture. He had the gentle persuasive manner of a Sunday School superintendent, and might have been outlining plans for a bank holiday excursion.

"A special responsibility will rest on the older boys," he seemed to be saying; "and as for the toddlers, everyone wants them to have a good time; but they must behave themselves properly if they're to make the best use of their visit to our Union." His voice was silky; and his lean cheeks were ribbed with auburn side-whiskers.

Cavendish thanked the captain for his inspiring address. "It is for us," he said, "more than a holiday. It is an education and an inspiration. Already, on this boat, we have felt ourselves to be in a different world; a better world; the world of the future. How different are the relations between officers and crew from any that we have known hitherto! How even the most menial tasks come to have dignity when stripped of all social and economic disqualifications! I have to thank the comrade captain and the comrades members of the crew for a delightful voyage and for an object lesson in how a liner should be run."

"Say something, fairy man," Mrs. Trivet whispered to Wraithby. He had nothing to say.

* * * * *

"This house," Ouspenski said, "was built by a rich merchant. Very bad taste, of course. Still, we are able to make use of it." Wraithby followed him from room to room; tall rooms, dimly lighted and hideous with coloured marble; gold fleurs-de-lis on a blue background. Frail gilt furniture was arranged against the walls; and glittering candelabra hung from the ceilings. Ouspenski loved the house, and showed it off more proudly and with more conviction than he had shown off the Dnieprostroi dam. The house was part of the Dictatorship of the Proletariat's inheritance, and so part of his.

In the centre of a black and white Japanese room stood a small table laid for dinner. Wraithby and Ouspenski sat down opposite one another, and underneath a candelabrum whose light brought to life the confused pattern of the walls. The pattern seemed in perpetual motion like a surface of dark water troubled by a steady wind. It seemed to ripple and pulsate.

Course followed course and drink followed drink. As his senses dissolved Wraithby felt himself becoming part of the Japanese room. The room's pulsating walls closed in on him; and he saw Ouspenski through a tremulous mist; as though far away; his voice dim and remote. He had not expected to make the acquaintance of the Dictatorship of the Proletariat in such a place and in such a way. "I want to ask you some questions," he said. Ouspenski's thick lips folded into a complacent smile. He was used to answering questions; and he thought he knew what the questions would be. Wraithby noticed the wave of his hair and smelt his scent.

"First, Who whom?"

Ouspenski was surprised. "When the Provisional Government fell," he intoned, "the power passed to the broad masses; that is, to the first Congress of Soviets. This became the Dictatorship of the Proletariat which, under the leadership of Comrade Stalin and the Communist party . . ."

"No, but seriously," Wraithby interrupted, "Who whom?"

Ouspenski's voice dropped confidentially. "The broad masses are like children. They need a father. A dictatorship of themselves. A force that is them but that, working apart from them, makes it possible for everything to be subordinated to their interests. Any other force must, by its very nature, deceive and enslave them. It alone . . ."

"Please," Wraithby pleaded, "Who whom?"

"I they," Ouspenski whispered.

Wraithby beamed. "Now I understand," he said.

"A German doctor who has been investigating the incidence of venereal disease in our Union," Ouspenski went on, anxious to forget his admission and to pass to more familiar ground, "reports that the position is highly satisfactory." His voice was impersonal. It came coldly out of space. Wraithby heard only fragments of what he said. In the gaps between these fragments he dozed.

"Infant mortality rate steadily decreasing. . . ."

"I don't say it's typical, but at a factory I visited the other day the workers told me they had everything they wanted except, perhaps, that there was a certain shortage of white bread. . . ."

"Everything done for the new generation. The children . . ."

Wraithby woke up with a start. "You they," he said. "I've got it right, haven't I?"

Ouspenski ignored his question and said, "I asked a few people to come and have coffee with us. Probably you know most of them."

They came running into the Japanese room. Girls

with fringes and high-waisted dresses. A gust of warm tweeds. Wraithby stood up on a chair. "Who whom?" he shouted. Then, pointing to Ouspenski, "He they."

"We've been seeing so much," they said eagerly. "We've seen factories and schools and hospitals and farms."

Cavendish, vibrant, went on alone. "It's not what's been achieved, or even what will be achieved. It's the spirit of the place. The feeling of brotherhood and determination. How invigorating it is! If I was a younger man I'd stay here. Live my life here. Bring up my children here."

"So should we if we were younger," they all agreed.

"I am younger and I'm staying," Wraithby said.

High in the wall a steel breast with a steel nipple began to blare out dance music. "Our radio," Ouspenski said, and took Anne into his arms, and began to dance. They all danced excitedly in the Japanese room with Wraithby standing on a chair and looking down on them. "Let's do our tableau again," he said. "Only the Dictatorship of the Proletariat, not Cavendish, must be God."

Ouspenski refused to be God. He thought they wanted to make him look ridiculous. Wraithby followed him from room to room trying to persuade him; from Japanese room to lady's boudoir, pale pink and white; from Gothic hall, where men in armour stood on pedestals, to velvet antechamber; through kitchens and lavatories, trying to persuade Ouspenski to be God.

"After all," he urged, "it's your right and your duty." At last, tired of the chase, he picked Ouspenski up in his arms and carried him, struggling, back to the Japanese room. He they, he thought; and I him. "Now," he said sternly, "play your part! Be God!" Ouspenski sat sullenly on his throne; and Wraithby and Mrs. Trivet cowered at his feet. "Speech!" they all shouted. "Speech!"

Cavendish clattered into the room in a suit of armour that he had put on in the hall. "I am God's flaming sword," he said. Ouspenski did not like the expression. He had heard it before on Ogpu anniversaries. "Let's stop," he protested, climbing down from his throne. "It's gone far enough."

* * * * *

Wraithby set out in quest of the real Russia. Everyone had impressed on him that at all costs he must make contact with the real Russia. He began with the theatre. There, he thought, I shall see this new vitality; these new standards of value, which constitute the real Russia, dramatically presented.

Sitting by Ouspenski's side in the front row of a theatre, he looked sideways at him; powdered and scented and curled; a dainty, spry Dictatorship of the Proletariat; barber or tourist guide or young man cautiously, experimentally, stealing an arm round a girl in cinema darkness.

On the stage was an observatory, glass-roofed, and, seen through the roof, searchlights coming and going. Two old men were huddled over a fire. Occasionally firing could be heard, and the sound of soldiers marching along a road outside. "The civil war," Ouspenski whispered. "Our victory." His eyes were bright with enthusiasm. He had seen the victory again and again in plays and ballets and films; but he never tired of it.

A Bolshevik soldier burst in on the two old men. He was rough and uncouth. His way of taking off his boots and his ignorance about astronomy provided comic relief. Wraithby was reminded of Barrie's plays. The soldier filled the same rôle as old-fashioned servants and policemen. Ouspenski's face, as he watched these antics, was full of kindly and complacent amusement; touched with pity, yet tender. "Not you they yet," Wraithby whispered.

"This is the conquest of power," Ouspenski said severely.

A Cheka officer, vigorous, upright, came to straighten matters up. The astronomer's lovely daughter hid behind her father's back when she saw the Cheka officer. His manliness and smart uniform and authoritative manner melted her adolescent heart; and she blushed and looked down on the ground. Ouspenski's mouth softened and moistened. "A pretty girl," he whispered to Wraithby.

In the next act the civil war was over; and the Bolshevik soldier, wearing a blue serge suit and a stiff collar, was installed as Communist director of the observatory. He shook hands warmly with a party of proletarian visitors, eager for astronomical information, who provided in the second act the same kind of comic relief that he had provided in the first. The aged astronomer lectured reluctantly to these visitors. His bourgeois prejudices were still unshed. "There's the whole theme of the play," Ouspenski whispered. "The conflict between the old ideas and the new."

"Which are old and which are new?" Wraithby asked.

"I don't know what you mean," Ouspenski answered haughtily.

The next act was the Cheka officer's office. He sat at a desk with a telephone at his elbow. The telephone rang constantly; and he shouted into it short emphatic orders. On the wall of the office was a huge graph of the Five-Year Plan showing the industrial production of other countries drooping down to nothing in black lines and the industrial production of Russia soaring up to infinity in a red line. The Cheka officer had by this time married the aged astronomer's lovely daughter. She came into his office from time to time dressed in a brown costume and carrying a music case. Her husband was very busy. He wore riding breeches and gaiters, and had grown a faint moustache since his first appearance.

Ouspenski explained to Wraithby that the astronomer had made an important discovery. A new planet was to appear in the sky in the near future. Unfortunately there was no telescope in Russia powerful enough to observe it; and the aged astronomer, out of spite, had sent his plans abroad. The ex-soldier and present Communist director was eager to get a telescope made in time. His Bolshevik impetuosity, however, was of no avail against the Cheka officer's argument that the factory concerned was fully employed at turning out binoculars for the Red Army. "You see," Ouspenski said, "it's a very exciting situation. No one knows what's going to happen. There's a conflict of loyalties." Ouspenski did not seem to be very excited. Nor did the audience.

In the event, a telescope was made in time for the planet's appearance. The factory was shown working overtime. "A striking scene," Ouspenski said. As a background there was the telescope draped with red flags; and in front six men hammered rhythmically at a bench. The Cheka officer delivered a long speech; and a table was arranged for a banquet. Wooden joints of meat and sides of bacon; pasteboard fishes and loaves of bread, caused a certain stirring in the audience. The aged astronomer looked ill at ease. He had on his conscience having sent his plans abroad.

The last act was back in the observatory. In a moving speech the aged astronomer confessed. He realised how wrong he had been. It was brought home to him that the, to him, tiresome proletarians were genuinely hungry for astronomical knowledge. He was converted, and, with limelight beating on his face, bore testimony to the excellence of the Dictatorship of the Proletariat. His lovely daughter fell into his arms; the Communist director wrung his hand; his arm rested on the shoulder of his son-in-law, the Cheka officer. At this moment of rejoicing and reconciliation an Ogpu orderly brought news that, after all, the plans had been stopped on the frontier. The curtain fell on the aged astronomer leading the singing of the "Internationale."

*   *   *   *   *

In the hotel restaurant they were all discussing the play. Next to Cavendish sat a Russian, red-cheeked and fat, and with distant beady eyes. "He's the author of the play," someone whispered to Wraithby. "A famous Soviet writer."

"Very remarkable play," Cavendish was saying. "The conflict going on in the astronomer's mind was brilliantly brought out. A serious play. The sort of play that in a capitalist society never gets produced." Insensibly he was working to a third of a column with so many words to a line.

"Back of it all," an American said, "was construction. Back of it all the great telescope; the machine. Back of it all workers giving of their best; tightening their belts, for the sake of an ideal."

"There's one question I should like to ask," Anne said, "about the relationship between the officer and the astronomer's daughter. Are we to understand that it was permanent, and that it precluded other relationships?"

"I take it," Cavendish answered, "that the relationship was, as it were, permanent for the time being, and that it didn't at all preclude . . ."

He looked at the famous Soviet writer, who nodded vaguely.

"It would have been better," Anne went on severely, "if that had been made clear by, for instance, the girl having a relationship with the soldier. As the play stands it's open to the criticism that it seems to accept, even idealise, a bourgeois view of marriage."

The famous Soviet writer suggested that they should all go with him to a little literary gathering at a friend's house. They agreed; and he took them to Paul Nollet's comfortable flat. It was in a building specially reserved for proletarian men-of-letters. Before becoming a proletarian man-of-letters Paul had been kept by a rich American. When she had gone native and discarded him for a negro he had turned to the Dictatorship of the Proletariat and laid his *vers libre* humbly at its feet. The *vers libre* had been appreciated; and he lived now in Moscow; a slight, dark man with a large nose and a pretty neck, spoilt looking and petulant, his eyes lazily restless, like a cow munching grass but always on the lookout for better pasture.

Cavendish stretched himself with a grunt on the floor. "I may be bourgeios," he seemed to be saying; "and a member of a bourgeois parliament with hopes of one day becoming an under-secretary of State; but at heart I'm on your side. I know the kind of behaviour the Dictatorship of the Proletariat expects of me when I'm on its premises." Wraithby found Paul's flat a home from home. The same cushions and books. The same pictures. The same bottles. The same people. One more farewell party, he thought bitterly. One more. A Spanish woman sitting on a sofa by herself bared her teeth at him. To protect himself he leant his head against the shoulder of a bare-legged Jewess.

Three of the girls with fringes and high-waisted dresses grouped themselves round Prince Alexis. He looked at them mournfully; a dark bearded man with a decaying mouth; savage and unhappy and lonely. "Tell us," the girls chanted together like school-children reciting a multiplication table, "how you, a prince, an aristocrat, became a Communist." Prince Alexis made noises in his stomach. How aristocratic he is! they thought. How interesting! How Russian!

"Yes, Prince," the American said, joining them, "my group in the States would be very interested to get your story." It was, the American thought, a tempting bait. He was fat and repellent; with several chins; a dramatic critic from Chicago.

Prince Alexis made more noises in his stomach. The girls' blond fringes drooping, Hawaiian, over their brows irritated him. The American's chins revolted him. He had no story for them. "I'm a Communist because of you," he said savagely. They were enchanted. "He's a Communist because of us," they murmured.

"Have I your permission, Prince, to repeat that to my group in the States?" the American asked.

"No," Prince Alexis answered.

The Dictatorship of the Proletariat was, to him, a principle; a law, that he believed in because it was exact. He had come to it at last as some debauchees come at last to join a religious order, or as some scientists and philosophers come at last to absorb themselves in the mathematics of the Old Testament. The more he had come to detest human beings the more attractive the Dictatorship of the Proletariat had seemed, because it alone opened out the possibility of clearing the world altogether of human beings and leaving only a principle existing, like electricity, in space. In the beginning was the Word, and in the end the Word, too. He wanted such an end.

The famous Soviet writer withdrew into Paul's bedroom, and dressed up in a silk kimono and a lace boudoir cap. Paul's complexion was uneasy. He looked shiftily at his mistress, who was stroking the hard bald head of a Russian in a leather coat. " Our association in Prague has joined the Communist party *en bloc*," he said. " I have written a poem in honour of the event." Leaning against the wall, legs and arms stretched out as though he was being crucified, he recited :

> " The Communist party; a force;
> A source of energy;
> Reshaping the world; men and women; societies;
> Living in me; in humanity;
> Irresistible; undying;
> A flame; a fire;
> Hope that destroys and recreates;
> The Communist party!"

The poem was received with applause; and the American asked if he might have the manuscript. " My group in the States," he said, " is very interested in all your literary innovations over here." Paul autographed and gave him the manuscript. " It will appear in tomorrow's *Pravda*," he said proudly. Wraithby thought that the poem was in the manner of Rabindranath Tagore. There was, when he came to think about it, a strong flavour of Tagore in the Dictatorship of the Proletariat's literary style.

* * * * *

He walked home with Prince Alexis. The streets were covered with snow; and what traffic and movement of people there was made no sound. In this silent town and amongst these silent people the play he had seen; the conversation he had listened to; the ideas rattling in his mind like dried peas in a peasecod, seemed trivial and empty. "I hate the Dictatorship of the Proletariat," he said; and disgust rose in him, choking him and making him incoherent. He saw the earth sprouting with life like flames, and Ouspenski hysterically beating at the flames while Cavendish and the others stood by; smiling; fatuous; complacent.

"Don't be a fool," Prince Alexis said.

"I hate the Dictatorship of the Proletariat," Wraithby repeated, knowing he was being ridiculous; not minding; "and so do you."

Prince Alexis stopped. His voice was pompous and dry. It rolled down the silent street prophesying wrath to come. "War soon. Europe falling into chaos. All except Russia. Then the great conquest which Marx and Lenin prophesied. Then the final victory."

After all, Wraithby thought, what is he but a man who's managed to be a parasite in three régimes? Aristocrat under Tzarism. Professor under capitalism. Proletarian man-of-letters under the Dictatorship of the Proletariat.

Wraithby knew that this lecture, academically delivered in a silent Moscow street, forced him to make a decision. He knew that he had reached an epoch in his life. There were two alternatives; clearly marked; unmistakable; and he had to choose between them. At that moment, and only for that moment, everything fitted into place. Every tendency in himself, in societies; the past and the future; all he had ever seen or thought or felt or believed, sorted itself out. It was a vision of Good and Evil. Heaven and Hell. Life and death. There were two alternatives; and he had to choose. He chose.

After choosing he felt gay, and brushed away the past as lightly as a spider's web. It was not in any case very substantial—cushions and empty glasses spread about here and there; in the grate a heap of cigarette ends; debris he'd accumulated. "Come and have a drink before you go home," he said to Prince Alexis.

The other dropped his voice. "Not a drink. But could you let me have a bath?"

He asked shyly for a bath.

"The fact is," he went on, "where I live there's no bathroom."

"Of course," Wraithby said.

He watched Prince Alexis dry himself. His body was white and tender like a boy's. The head; so battered and decayed, did not seem to belong to it; like an old worn hood on a new motor-car. All the wear and tear of living seemed to have gone into the head, leaving the rest of his body fresh and new.

"Do you really believe," Wraithby asked, "that these awful plays are good; these wretched people happy; these revolting Jews, great leaders and prophets; these decrepit buildings, fine architecture; these dingy slums, new socialist cities; these empty slogans bawled mechanically, a new religion; these stale ideas (superficial in themselves and even then misunderstood), the foundation and hope of the future?"

"You don't understand in the least," Prince Alexis said, drying himself slowly as though reluctant to cover up his body and leave only his stained head exposed. "You're a fool. Plays and people and leaders and buildings and slogans have nothing to do with it. They don't matter in the least."

"What does matter then?"

The bathroom had no windows. Steam hung in it. It might have been a remote cave. Or just space. "The inevitability of it all. The fact that it had to happen. Forces interacting and producing a resultant force. The fulfilment of the law and the prophets."

In the beginning was the Word, and in the end the Word, too.

* * * * *

It seemed to Wraithby that Lenin's tomb must be real Russia; and so he visited it often. There was always a queue straggling across the Red Square. As he moved towards the entrance of the tomb he looked at the people moving with him. What were they thinking? What were they hoping? Their faces were expressionless; their movements mechanical; their voices, when they spoke, quiet. In the Red Square ghosts; in the tomb shadows. Like shadows they passed by the glass case containing the Dictatorship of the Proletariat's embalmed head.

The atmosphere in the tomb was damp and stale. It smelt like a cloakroom in an elementary school on a wet day. The head inside its glass case was fungoid;

fresh and vivid like a fungus growing in darkness; unwholesome like a fungus; soft and poisonous. Beard and finger-nails were trimmed. The head required attention. Was it done ceremonially? Wraithby wondered. Lords and ladies of the bedchamber coming secretly to brush the hair and comb the beard and polish the nails of their Dictatorship; to pose the head to the best advantage on its red pillow; to rearrange the brown tunic and pin new ribbon on its breast. Were consecrated scissors and file kept for the purpose? Holy water used?

Of all the symbols that had ever been set up to intimidate and inspire, this little embalmed man seemed to Wraithby the most revolting. Even the preserved bodies of Pharaohs were hidden away secretly, and looking on them made a crime. Even spiritualists were content with taps and voices, and left the body itself to be consumed by fire or to rot underground. Even Christians satisfied themselves with eating and drinking Christ, and with grovelling before fragments of his cross or a phial of his blood. Their living Christ was ethereal; but the living Lenin was dead Lenin embalmed and brushed and manicured.

Wraithby drifted into an anti-religious museum with Anne. It had once been a cathedral. An enormous pendulum hung from its dome, and swung gently backwards and forwards demonstrating the diurnal revolution of the earth. A few people were watching it. "Very impressive," Anne said. "Excellent propaganda. Instead of the mumbo-jumbo of religion a clean scientific principle being demonstrated."

"Dearest," Wraithby answered, kissing her hand (soon she would be gone and he never have to live with her again), "it's not impressive at all. You might as well say it was impressive to crucify Einstein instead of Christ."

She had a pink face with cropped blond hair, and was studying languages. Already she knew three languages.

"Your whole attitude is silly," she said, and thought. Poor old Wraith! He'll never do anything. How nice he is though! He remembered having seen her in the sidecar of a motor-bicycle driven by a bio-chemist named Simon, and how her head, sticking out of the sidecar, had seemed like part of its works; an extra cylinder, and how the sight of her then had given him a chill of fear and foreboding like the sight of Kronstadt.

"Or you might as well say," he went on, "that the spectacle of you and Simon making love here under this dome would be impressive as demonstrating a clean scientific principle instead of mumbo-jumbo."

He laughed gleefully, seeing them, in the throes of lust, being anti-religious propaganda.

Anne turned away. "You'll marry Simon?" he asked.

"Marry!" she answered contemptuously.

"I mean be with him. Have a relationship with him. Live with him."

"Simon," she said, "is coming to Russia to do bio-chemical research; and I'll come with him, and study Russian."

"I'm glad," Wraithby said. "You'll be happy together here."

He saw the others off at the station. They really are going now, he thought, and knew it was too late. After all they'd been right. They were the Dictatorship of the Proletariat; and, flying from them, he'd flown to them. Cavendish leaned out of the window. "How I envy you, Wraith! How I envy you!" He was on fire to get back to London, and to write articles and make speeches.

Wraithby smiled wanly. At least he knew them; and now they were going and he would be left alone. "Good-bye! Good-bye!" he shouted, and whispered to Anne, hate making his voice husky and sincere, "It's been lovely, dearest. I shan't forget." The train moved slowly out of the station, Cavendish still leaning out of the window. It moved away, leaving emptiness behind it.

They at least had something to fall back on; their own falsity; their own egotism driving them to type words, and make speeches, and accumulate bank balances, and toady; their own stupidity, a protection, a source of strength. He had nothing. A melancholy absurd figure; tall; mouth sagging open; disintegrated body matching disintegrated soul, he turned forlornly from the platform, knowing that it was himself he had watched steam slowly away, and that the emptiness left behind was in his own heart.

* * * * *

He tramped about day after day looking for a room

in the real Russia; passing through buildings alive with human beings as with vermin; human beings packed densely together and forming a paste. "Are you ever alone?" he asked a woman. "Sometimes," she said, "I long even to be sent to Siberia because there at least I'd be alone." He had foreign money to pay for a room. It was tempting; and offers were made to push back a little further the flood of human beings; wall off a little space; build a dam behind which he could live. He refused these offers. Here and there he found whole flats occupied by Communist officials or by members of the Ogpu. Oases of luxury like his hotel.

A Bulgarian barber helped him in his search. He was a young man who had lived for ten years in Chicago. A belted tweed overcoat, his initials on the buckle, and wide-bottomed trousers that overhung his shoes, were a relic of this time. Also a photograph in a leather case of himself on a spree with his girl in the country. "She's swell," he said when he showed the photograph to Wraithby.

"How do you like it here?" Wraithby asked.

He looked up quickly like an animal; eyes afraid and alert.

"I sleep with de boys. Ten in a room, and not much eats."

As he waited for a meal to be served in the hotel restaurant his saliva overflowed.

"I was in partnership with my uncle," he went on between bites; "but dey wouldn't give me American nationality. I'd come in over de Canadian frontier for two hundred and fifty dollars. Chicago . . ."

His dark eyes melted at the thought of Chicago; and he pulled out his photograph and looked at it.

Wandering about in this teeming misery; looking for a corner of it to live in, Wraithby understood the difference between ideas and reality. He understood that every sort of idea was an unreal simplification. Reality flooded into his mind like light, revealing there a litter of ideas. He swept away this litter; and his mind was clean but empty. "After all," he heard himself saying; lounging on coloured cushions; drinking hot tea and eating buttered toast, "there are worse things in life than starving." That was an idea. In reality there was nothing worse than starving. It was an ultimate misery. "I went to see 'Uncle Vanya' the other day," a Russian said to him; "and I wondered what they were all bothering about since they'd got plenty to eat."

The litter of ideas in his own mind was the litter of ideas outside. Rootless, unreligious ideas. What a blight they had been! Piling up into shadows whose darkness cloaked a reversion to savagery. Piling up into a Dictatorship of the Proletariat. Howled out of loud-speakers. American bathing girls with ideas tattooed on their bottoms. Triple portrait by the Kremlin wall; Lenin on the left; Marx in front; Stalin on the right. "After all," he heard himself saying; lying in bed by Anne's side, "the family has to be abolished. Property has to be abolished. Otherwise . . ." In a warm bed, in darkness, he had abolished the family and property. The Dictatorship of the Proletariat had also abolished the family and property. Now he wandered amongst the teeming misery that was left looking for a corner of it to live in.

          *   *   *   *   *

Wraithby was not surprised to find Bramwell Smith and a Jewess sitting in the hotel lounge one evening. It was inevitable that Bramwell Smith should some time or other find his way to Moscow. "You'll be happy here," he said, "and appreciated here. It's just the place for you." Bramwell Smith told him that he was off to the Krimea. His small, blond, acute head was fastened on to his body without a neck. As he spoke his fingers splayed over the Jewess's knee. "Doris and Olga and Derwent and the children are coming out, too," he said. Already he saw himself advising the Dictatorship of the Proletariat; finger on its pulse; head cocked on one side; prescribing. "And you?" he asked.

"I hate it," Wraithby said.

"Some people can't see beneath the blunders and mistakes," the Jewess murmured.

"I know," Wraithby said. "Back of this and back of that."

"I felt bad myself when I first came," she went on. "Little things annoyed me. For instance, it annoyed me that they couldn't make beds. It got on my nerves so that I thought I'd have to leave. Now it doesn't any more. Isn't it queer that they can't make beds?"

Like Muskett, she had her grievance against the Dictatorship of the Proletariat.

"Why do you hate it?" Bramwell Smith asked.

"Not," Wraithby answered, "because they're starving; or because they live in filthy nearness to one another; or because their lives are dull and unhappy; or because of the din of monotonous, shoddy propaganda; or because the bosses are megalomaniac fools and the rest terrorised into imbecility; or because you like it. In its very texture something absurd and trivial and barbarous. Every stale idea vomited up again. Everything that you believe in and that I hate. All the dingy hopes that have echoed and re-echoed over Europe for a century and now are spent. The poor little frightened soul of the Dictatorship of the Proletariat is what I despise. Not its works."

"Supposing two or three million peasants do die this winter," the Jewess said mechanically, getting up. "What of it?"

She was off to a lecture on the Film and the Class Struggle. As she revolved with the revolving hotel doors, red lips flashing like a lighthouse lamp, Wraithby understood pogroms.

"No, but look here," Bramwell Smith said, "the men I saw this morning in the Commissariat for Heavy Industry—they seemed very nice; very capable; very intelligent. They were very ready to learn. Very ready to take my advice."

Wraithby remembered him as an undergraduate organising mixed discussion groups on Freud; in a laboratory, white-coated, patrolling up and down a row of test-tubes; reciting one sultry August evening; stretched out on his belly on the floor, drinking thin tea, the tale of his loves. "I tell you," he said again, "that you'll be happy here. There's everything you want here."

* * * * *

He sat over a meal looking at Claud Mosser. "The newness of it! That's what I like," Mosser said. A world fit for Mosser to live in. "Look at their prison system. Look at their divorce laws. Look at their courts and their schools and their crèches. Back of it all, youth. The ardour and courage of youth. Outsiders may be shocked; even repelled. But they've got to respect the flaming courage of youth that's back of it all."

"The only thing I like about Bolshevism," Wraithby said, "is its antiquity. There's nothing older than Bolshevism. It takes you back to the beginning of time. Before history. Before animal life. Before matter had any shape. It takes you back to when the universe was a chaos of energy."

Mosser saw that there was sales resistance to be overcome. He eased his cuffs and smoothed down his waistcoat.

"Look at the way they've abolished prostitution," he said. "Why, I was reading the other day in a book by Maurice Hindus a description of a home for reformed prostitutes. Listen to this. Can you beat it?"

He took the book out of his pocket and began to read:

> "As you go into this house now you are greeted by a man who offers to check your coat and rubbers. . . . This gives you a feeling that the place

has a dignity of its own, like a theatre or an opera house. . . . A place of no small consequence, then. . . . This feeling heightens as you mount the freshly painted stairway and enter the office. . . . A young man of about thirty is at the desk. . . . He wears a modern suit of clothes, complete with collar and tie, and, what is more astonishing, spats. . . . Communist though he is, he deems it essential to keep up as presentable an appearance as the scanty supplies in the Moscow haberdashery shops permit."

"No, I can't beat it," Wraithby said.

"Think of the way prostitutes are treated in other countries," Mosser went on. "Outcasts. The lowest of the low. And here—check your coat and rubbers; freshly painted stairway; young man with collar, tie and, what is more astonishing, spats."

His face glowed with enthusiasm. "Where else would you find such an institution?" The idea stirred him; a genuine romantic, like the idea of a king or a president or a prime minister taking tea in a humble cottage. "Mrs. Peabody bobbed a curtsey and without any embarrassment asked His Majesty whether he took one lump or two." "A building once perhaps the home of one of the Tzar's mistresses; now houses prostitutes. Outcasts. The lowest of the low," he went on.

They went together to the circus. The attendants were dressed in gold uniforms, now shabby. It was a ghost of a circus; the animals aged; the apparatus battered; the performers jaded. "Back of it all, youth. The ardour and courage of youth," Wraithby whispered to Mosser. Was this the real Russia? A circus whose splendour had faded. No change except that its energy was spent. Nothing new about the circus except its disorder and shabbiness. The horses did their tricks stiffly like old men kneeling down in church; and the trainer's whip cracked without conviction.

"This is the past," Mosser whispered back. "In process of being liquidated. Sad, perhaps; but necessary. The past being cleared away."

"Where do I find the present?" Wraithby asked.

"Out in the factories; in the great collective farms; in the theatres with their living revolutionary art; in concerts where workers meet to listen to the best music, afterwards to discuss . . ."

His question set Mosser off on to a great tirade. He fled from Mosser. The enemy, he thought; the destroyer, more dangerous and terrible because he deems it essential to keep up as presentable an appearance as the scanty supplies in the Moscow haberdashery shops permit.

At a concert Wraithby heard a tall, elderly negress sing. Her little blond husband, face pink and shining, accompanied her on the piano. He wore evening dress, shirt badly laundered, trousers and coat shiny with wear. The negress's voice was cracked. She sang Indian Love Lyrics, and then Songs of the Hebrides, and then Negro Spirituals. A pianist in a dress suit, Wraithby thought, remembering Mosser, complete with white bow and waistcoat, and, most surprising of all, patent leather shoes. A concert of some consequence, then.

He took the negress and her husband out to supper. Though she was old and falling to pieces there was something vivid and likable about her. Decaying, Wraithby thought, but not disintegrating; not disintegration in spats; not disintegration of some consequence. Her thick mouth was folded sadly and her black eyes were desperate. "I loved your singing," Wraithby said untruthfully. She smiled; and, when she had drunk some wine, said, "My voice is going. There's something wrong with my throat." Every now and again she coughed huskily. "When I came to Russia twenty-five years ago . . ."

"Twenty-five years?"

"Yes, one of the Grand Dukes fetched me over. He heard me sing in New York. They made a great fuss of me."

Wraithby saw her black neck gleaming with jewels; tireless at midnight parties; energy making her indifferent to champagne; emptying her admirers of their appetites; a virgin amongst them; everlasting virginity.

"You had fun? You enjoyed yourself?"

She nodded. It set her apart, Wraithby thought. It made her sublime. He and the little blond husband looked up at her adoringly because she had dared to enjoy herself.

A gipsy band was playing on a raised platform. Its shrill incoherent music filled the restaurant. A gipsy girl quivered to the music, each part of her body trembling, yet so perfectly that her body seemed still. "We'll dance," Wraithby said. He and the negress danced. The music, and the wine, and his admiration for her, made her forget her unhappiness and be young again. "We'll outlive the Dictatorship of the Proletariat," Wraithby said. "Even if we die we'll outlive it." He saw the shallowness of Prince Alexis's prophecy. His voice, booming down a silent Moscow street, was the emptiest sound of all. He saw the shallowness of his own fear and indignation. Supposing all that Prince Alexis prophesied came to pass; supposing there came chaos of some consequence; supposing Mosser rode the storm in spats, and he was submerged; even then life remained, like a spore, with its protective covering; waiting perhaps for centuries; at last shooting out roots, growing. "You and I and the gipsies'll outlive the Dictatorship of the Proletariat," he repeated. The negress smiled without understanding what he meant. "Some of them are quite nice boys," she said. "Rough but nice. Parties in the Kremlin are quite like old times."

* * * * *

Wraithby moved out to a remote suburb of Moscow, where he lived in a wooden house. There were long avenues of fir trees nearby, and a dilapidated park of Culture and Rest. Cardboard tractors, and slogans and graphs, faded and weather-beaten, flapped in the wind. He walked up and down these avenues every day until he was tired, and then went back to the wooden house to write. It was easy for him to write. He had only to take his life piece by piece and destroy it; hold each fragment up to the light and watch it shrivel away to nothing. It was a dry life that burnt easily; flaming and crackling and smoking like withered gorse on a common.

A party of German Jews sometimes drove out to the

next-door house. They were fat, jolly men who played ball and did exercises in the garden. After dinner they would light their cigars, and drink a liqueur or two, and put on the gramophone. The Dictatorship of the Proletariat was irrelevant as far as they were concerned. They had their motor-cars and their girl friends, and did business in Moscow. In all conceivable circumstances, Wraithby thought, they'll have motor-cars and girl friends and do business. Like empire-builders who dress for dinner in the jungle they preserved their standards in Mr. Aarons's Soviet Union; hair glossy; girls slim and blond and elegant; business lucrative; motor-cars swift and tidy; bright toecaps peeping, like buds, out of the foliage of a spat. These, Wraithby thought, are a constant. They survive everything. He liked them.

An electric train carried him to and from Moscow. Pressed against people; swaying with them to the movement of the train; pushing through them to get out; running, part of a ferocious army, from the station to the platform with an incoherent loud-speaker bawling in his ears; fighting on and off tram-cars, Ouspenski's promised land seemed remote. We'll all outlive the Dictatorship of the Proletariat, he thought. Even if we die we'll outlive it.

He searched painstakingly for the real Russia; up and down boulevards where children skated and played, and where old decrepit men stood with their cameras offering to photograph passers-by against a sea-front, or in a cardboard motor-car, or sitting on the painted steps of a marble palace; in cinemas and libraries and museums and shops and government offices and clubs and restaurants; by the frozen river and amongst the pages of newspapers. Perhaps, he thought, there is no real Russia. Only an organisation and organised force existing like sign-posts and barbed-wire fences in a stretch of wild country; only statistics and slogans shouted from the Kremlin and then lost in space; only waves of showmanship that pile up to wash a Bernard Shaw or a Lord Edderton or a Mrs. Trivet over Russia. Was Mosser real Russia? Was Ouspenski real Russia? They danced, bespatted; consequential, on the surface of reality for a little while like company promoters and intimate biographers and film stars. With Jefferson hanging on to their skirts they got away with this and that for a little while. Then reality engulfed them. He saw Mosser and Ouspenski and Nollet and Mrs. Eardley-Wheatsheaf and Mrs. Trivet and Lord Edderton dancing on Russia; leaving footprints—famine, terror, heavy industry—but not really touching Russia. It was beyond their reach.

When he went to see Bulgakov, a Ukrainian with a round, wistful face that still seemed full of sun, Wraithby generally took a bottle of wine in his pocket. He and Bulgakov and Bulgakov's wife would talk together in whispers, because three children were sleeping in a corner of the room. If he got a little tipsy Bulgakov talked about the Ukraine. "You should go there," he whispered. "Even now, when there's no food. It's a lovely country. Even now. But before . . ." He cracked his finger-joints and described how happy life had been once in the Ukraine. "Of course, we didn't think it was particularly happy then; but I can see now . . ." His wife, fearing an outburst that would wake the children and perhaps be overheard, changed the subject.

"Won't you have some Soviet cake?" she said, fetching out part of a loaf of black bread; the only food they had.

"Happy," Bulgakov went on, "because our lives were connected with something. The poorest. The wretchedest. There were occasions in the year; Christmas; Easter; marriages and funerals. Based on absurd superstitions, perhaps, and on absurd social customs. But gay."

Now, Wraithby thought, a pendulum swinging ponderously backwards and forwards, and demonstrating the diurnal revolution of the earth. A live superstition replaced by a dead one.

Bulgakov pointed at three pictures on his walls. They were by a peasant. One was of five solemn men with heavy black moustaches sitting at a table and drinking; one of a bearded priest on a donkey with an umbrella over his shoulder, and one of a squat child garlanded with flowers.

"You see what I mean," Bulgakov said.

It was the first proletarian art Wraithby had seen in Russia. He remembered the picture galleries he'd been through with their fatuous notices:

> "These twelfth century ikons mark the early stages of the struggle between kulaks and big landowners."

"In Rubens the development of capitalism reaches a decisive phase, and the toiling masses realise their decisive rôle";

and the heavy portraits of Soviet personalities; glaring and lifeless as portraits of Christ in newly-founded Asiatic churches; and the pretentious machine-cult posters that Mrs. Trivet took home to hang in her drawing-room.

"Yes, I see what you mean," he said to Bulgakov.

The only place he could find on the train going back was on the little iron platform between one carriage and another. Just before the train started a man carrying a box joined him there. He was short, with a peaked face and three or four days' growth of blond stubble on his chin. Also, he was drunk. They went rocking through the snow; icy cold; the distances between stations getting longer and longer, until there were stretches of whiteness and clusters of black trees. The man lolled on his box, and seemed unaware that his position was precarious. He even dropped off to sleep. Wraithby, anxious for his safety, nudged him and asked, "How's life?"

The man looked up curiously like an elf; head on one side; eyebrows raised. "When there's bread I eat it; and when there isn't, I starve."

Another, Wraithby thought, who'll outlive the Dictatorship of the Proletariat. "The Revolution . . ." he began. The man growled angrily and spat. Wraithby reached across the little iron platform and hugged him. Arms round one another and shouting, they went rocking through the snow from one station to another.

The road from Wraithby's station led up past a row of wooden houses; then by a little church coloured pale blue and gold; then through a copse of trees; smooth snow untouched and gleaming in the moonlight. Passengers from the train distributed themselves in the wooden houses; not speaking; moving silently; black figures on white snow. Real Russia? Wraithby wondered, and began to run; his blood warm and his face glowing, and happiness like a fire inside him.

*   *   *   *   *

Wraithby fell asleep in an old-fashioned sleeping-car. He woke up, and, peeping through the window, saw a wide sweep of country. It gave him a great sense of relief; and he realised that Moscow was sombre and shut in, and that the dreary propaganda that unceasingly washed over it had been oppressing his spirits. Now he saw a horizon again. Stalin on Leninism, he thought; Lenin on Stalinism; Molotov on Molotovism. Pah!

He went from place to place and found an intenser and more passionate and simpler misery than in Moscow. In a German settlement, a little oasis of prosperity in a collectivised wilderness, he watched peasants asking for bread. They wanted to be admitted to the settlement. They knelt down and wept and pleaded. Whatever else I may do or think in the future, he thought, I must never pretend that I haven't seen this. Ideas will come and go; but this is more than an idea. It is peasants kneeling down in the snow and asking for bread. Something I have seen and understood.

The Germans showed him their settlement. They walked with him through pig-sties, stirring up one fat pig after another. They caught sheep between their legs and parted the wool to show him its thickness. They spread grain over the palms of their hands, and gingerly opened the stables of horses and bulls. Their scarred faces, cruel and clumsy, were sensitive to the nature of fertility. They brought the smell of fertility to his nostrils. Barbarians, too, he thought; but belonging to the earth. The barbarity of Mosser and of the Dictatorship of the Proletariat was abstract.

In the evening the Germans put a military march on their gramophone. They all stood up; stiffly; absurdly, spurred heels clicking together, faces obtusely solemn. A barbarism, Wraithby thought, that may, and probably will, make war on civilisation. Not, like the Dictatorship of the Proletariat, on life.

He walked through the streets of Rostov with an elderly Intourist guide. Her face was crumpled into a perpetual smile. A bib with a collar attached covered her chest and neck. They had been together to a tractor factory, and to various buildings; some completed and some uncompleted. She had been showing him over Ouspenski's promised land; demonstrating the general idea.

"How do you like our Union?" she asked; an elderly spinster who ought to have been serving tea; putting the cosy on the pot between one cup and another, instead of demonstrating the general idea. An elderly spinster whose store of bibs had lasted since the Revolution. For fifteen years.

"Not very much," he answered gently.

"I get meat three times a week," she went on.

"I'm glad," he said.

"And then we women are free."

She said it very quietly. "We women are free." Her triumph was unassertive. She used, Wraithby thought, to attend meetings in connection with the emancipation of women. She used to demand the vote. Sowing the wind. Such a little piping wind! And now the whirlwind, bringing her meat three times a week and leaving undisturbed her store of bibs.

"I'm glad," he said, "that you women are free."

He left her and turned into a church. A service was going on with quite a large congregation, mostly peasants. A melancholy passionate service. Religion was a refuge from the Dictatorship of the Proletariat. Priests in vestments and with long hair were chanting prayers; little candle flames lighting the darkness, and incense rising. The voices of the priests were dim like echoes, and the congregation curiously quiet; curiously still. Wraithby found their stillness hopeful; even exhilarating. It suggested that even general ideas spent themselves at last and were nothing.

The priests moved down amongst the congregation, swinging censers; their faces battered and frail; people kneeling and crossing themselves before them. They had been purified by suffering. Their spirits had been strengthened and made to burn steadily by it. They had proved strong enough to keep intact a link with the past. When they passed near him, Wraithby, unbelieving, knelt and gratefully received their blessing.

Later in the evening he dined with representatives of the Rostov Soviet and of the Rostov Press and of the Rostov Vox. A little Jew with long hair and a crumpled shirt front took the head of the table. "We had Sir Webb here the other day," he said. "Such a nice man!" They ate and drank cheerfully together. The little Jew never let the cognac bottle stray far out of his reach. He had been a political exile in Germany. "Ask us questions," he said to Wraithby.

Wraithby had no more questions to ask. He knew all he wanted to know about the Dictatorship of the Proletariat. He felt, however, that something was expected of him. "About agriculture?" he began.

Everyone spoke at once. He could distinguish phrases here and there. "Sown area increased by forty per cent. . . . wall newspapers . . . spring sowing campaign . . . As the factories in 1920, so now the farms . . ."

When the noise had abated, he said, "Thank you. Now I understand." He wanted to ask them, "Boys, dearest boys, are you sure that the parallel is correct? Factories and land? Isn't agriculture somehow more sensitive? Lending itself less to statistical treatment? Will peasants whose lives have been torn up by the roots make things grow even if you drive them into the fields at the end of a bayonet?" But he knew that it was as impossible to argue against a general idea as against an algebraic formula. So instead he said, "Ask me some questions."

Coyly; head on one side; wagging a finger, the little Jew asked, "When will the revolution come in England?"

Wraithby, too, was coy; he wagged a finger. "'Who knows?"

"And why doesn't Lloyd George come to Russia?"

He wanted to leave them happy. They'd been very friendly and sociable; and he wanted to part from them in a cheerful happy atmosphere. "I'll tell you a secret," he said. "He is coming. And soon. In a month or so."

Their faces were radiant. "Lloyd George coming? Really coming?"

He assured them again and again that he was really coming. Sir Webb and then Lloyd George! It seemed too good to be true.

* * * * *

The future seemed empty to Wraithby. It was easy to burn up the past; but not so easy to face a future lacking everything that had given the past substance. Even for him; a person of no importance; a nobody, the patterns he'd made and unmade in his mind meant something. They'd at least filled up a certain space. They'd at least given him an occupation. Now, he thought, my occupation's gone. Ambition stirred painfully in the emptiness he'd made inside himself; and with adolescent morbidity he began to long to die.

To die! he would whisper to himself. To cease upon the midnight with no pain! feeling that this Dictatorship of the Proletariat, this promised land, this general idea, was everywhere; in his own soul. Layer upon layer of chaos folding one on the other like petals, he thought; and at the very core, myself; a chaos. The future was a sweep of grey time to him because he had seen the reality whose distorted shadow had been his past.

Before leaving Moscow he went to say good-bye to Blythe; an Englishman who'd come to live in Moscow with his wife and three children. He worked in a factory. Skin was drawn so tightly over his face that it was like a skull. His expression was mean and unpleasant. Wraithby liked and respected him more than anyone else he'd met in Russia.

"I thought you'd be going soon," Blythe said enviously; bitterly.

"Would you like to go, then?"

"I can't go, so the question doesn't arise."

Wraithby knew that Blythe had no foreign money, and that he'd been somehow persuaded to take Soviet nationality. He also knew that the family was starving since Blythe only earned two hundred roubles a month and got very little besides bread on his ration card.

"I'm here for good."

"I've got a little money. I'll lend you enough to get you back to England."

"What'd I do then?" Blythe asked, his voice angry and bitter. His face was scarred with the fight to get money that he'd had to carry on all his life. The need for money had dried up his skin and pulled it tightly over his face.

"Do you wish you hadn't come?"

"I don't know whether I wish I hadn't come or not;

but I admit to feeling angry about the lies that brought me here. Articles in a magazine by Bernard Shaw; on glossy paper; illustrated. An aunt sent them to me."

He looked round at his room; in a basement and with one small window.

"I wish," he went on, "that he could be made to come and live here, and change his money into roubles, and take Soviet nationality."

"It's a ghastly business, isn't it?"

"Ghastly failure. Ghastly misunderstanding. Ghastly betrayal. But I don't mind that. To me the thing's justified because of its beginnings. Because for a little while the masses stirred, became coherent, dominant. What had to happen, happened; and nothing can ever alter the fact that it happened, or that, in happening, it made the world different. All the same, when I think of that absurd, vain, rich old man letting himself be gulled; accepting the betrayal; spreading it in his magazine articles, and fetching us here to starve, I long for the same thing to happen in England if only so that he and his like might suffer the same fate they've suffered here."

Wraithby knew the streets in Salford where Blythe had grown up. He knew the newspapers he'd read, and the unemployment exchange where he'd waited, and the co-operative stores where he'd bought food, and the men he'd voted for.

"It never did happen really," he said. "It was a betrayal, a fraud, from the beginning. Do you remember how, when Trotsky and the others went to negotiate the Treaty of Brest Litovsk, they took with them six workers and six peasants? The six workers and peasants were given rooms and meals. They just stayed there and took no part in the negotiations. They were just a façade; a sham. It's been like that the whole way through."

"Perhaps so," Blythe said. "But I don't think so. I think there was a moment, very short, very soon passed, when Lenin and his miserable crew were servants, not masters. That moment was the most important so far in the history of the human race."

Blythe walked along with Wraithby. They paused in the Red Square. "You know more about this business than anyone else," Wraithby said. "I mean how it works and what it means to people. If you came back to England you could write about it. After all, you haven't looked at the thing. You've suffered it."

"I'd never write about it," Blythe said. "I'd have to attack it; and I'd never do that." He pointed to Lenin's tomb. "You can't understand what I felt when I saw them standing there, and the Red Army filing past, and the aeroplanes overhead, and the great procession, and the tanks and armoured cars."

"I think I can. You mean it was you standing there."

"Exactly."

"That's the difference. I didn't see myself standing there."

"Besides," Blythe said, "they'd never give me a passport out."

Blythe went home; and Wraithby continued walking round the Red Square by himself. Two peasants and a child were huddled under a doorway. Soldiers with fixed bayonets were on guard outside Lenin's tomb. Suddenly he noticed a change in the wind that was blowing against his face. It was touched with warmth. It was fragrant. Suddenly spring had begun. The frozen river would thaw, and sun make the earth bare; then green. Thus it had happened a million times before. Thus it would happen a million times again. Nothing could prevent this process taking place—the sudden, unexpected coming of spring. Wraithby took in great breaths of the warm fragrant air.

THE END